BATTLE AT THE GALACTIC JUNKYARD

CHARLES RAY

U2S
hurd pres

North Potomac, MD

This book is a work of fiction. Names, descriptions, places, and incidents are products of the author's imagination, or are used fictionally. Any resemblance to actual events or persons, living or dead, is purely coincidental.

For information about this and other works of this author, contact the author at charlesray.author@yahoo.com.

Printed in the United States of America.

ISBN: 0692414797
ISBN-13: 978-0692414798

ONE

His head was pounding and his mouth felt like someone had poured a bucket of finely ground gravel down his throat. Cullen Park sat hunched over the table in the Rusty Bucket Saloon, a flagon of guggle melon juice between his large hands and a plate of fried saurofowl to the side. Every time the odor from the bits of brown meat reached his nose, he had to fight the urge to spew the contents of his stomach across the table. He knew, though, that as bad as he felt, if he did that, he would feel considerable worse. Bitsy, his assistant, did not like being puked on. The last person to do something like that to Bitsy Jacobs had needed sixty stitches to close the gash she'd put in his head.

"You really should eat something," Bitsy said. "It might make you feel better."

Cullen groaned. "The only thing that will make me feel better right now is dying."

"That's what you get for trying to drink a liter of juju juice."

"Hah, that shows what you know," Cullen said. "I didn't *try* to drink a liter, I *drank* a liter."

She shook her head, her blonde locks flying back and forth over bright blue eyes. "I rest my case. You're not just plain stupid, you're supremely, and complicatedly stupid."

"Oh, not so loud, would you? My head's killing me."

"Eat the damn saurofowl," she said. "It'll make you feel better, I promise."

He looked across the table at her. Bitsy had been his assistant at the repair yard going on two years now, and she was smart—and stubborn—so she probably was right. Besides, he thought, if he didn't eat the damn stuff, she'd never stop yakking at him.

Even though he was nominally the owner and chief mechanic at Park's Parts Emporium, the largest repair facility on End of the Line, Bitsy ran rings around him in her ability to diagnose and fix ship engines and just about anything else that ran or flew. She was also as tough as plasteel with the temper of a ding boar when pissed off.

Cullen had inherited the place from his father, Jubilee Park, who had inherited it from his father, Tongsu 'Tony' Park, who had founded it way back when the first settlement was established on the planet that had, until that time, been known only as M1369X, and that name only to a few diehard astronavigators who liked to pore over maps of remote sectors of the Solar System, because it was in a region not normally visited by space ships on legitimate business.

Tony Park had led the first group of settlers, eight women and twenty-four men, and was still considered End of the Line's founding father, a legacy that Cullen was determined to live down.

Not that he was called on to live *up* to it. Given the male-female imbalance in the population, it had been decided that each woman would have three husbands, which eventually led to a matriarchal social lash up that persisted. The current leader of End of the Line was Moira Nakitomi. Moira was the daughter of Nobu Nakitomi and Elvira Park. Elvira was the daughter of Tony Park and Esther Merriweather, making her Cullen's cousin to some degree. He'd never been too interested in math, or his distant relations, so he wasn't sure, and Moira disliked him with a passion, so he was never motivated to figure out the relationship.

Cullen put a spoonful of the meat in his mouth. Brown gravy dripped down his chiseled chin. "Hmph foh guf, than gyu," he said.

"Stop talking with food in your mouth," Bitsy said. "You're spewing food all over the table. You know how Moira hates that."

He swallowed. "I said, this is good, thank you," he said. "And, I don't really give a flark what Moira likes or doesn't like."

"Yeah, right . . . but, seriously, though, you

don't want her raising your assessment, do you?"

The colony leader was also the tax collector, and Cullen knew that getting on her bad side could result in a change in what he was required to pay, which in his opinion was already far too much. Only members of the colony council were exempt from paying assessment—making up for the fact that they served without salary.

"Okay, okay . . . I'll be nice. Now, as soon as I finish my breakfast, we got that cargo ship jump engine to fix. Did you find an anti-matter coil?"

"Yes, in fact," she said. "There was one in that pile of junk in the back of the lot. Just needed the rust scraped off. I'll have it installed before lunch."

The saurofowl didn't stop the headache, but it did settle his stomach, so Cullen was able to make his way to the yard without having to stop and hurl his stomach contents into the nearest gutter. His head, however, throbbed with each step on the dusty street from the Rusty Bucket to Park's Parts Emporium. Bitsy, for a change, walked in silence, for which he was supremely grateful.

The owner of the cargo ship, one Oswald Jenkins, was waiting for them at the locked gate. A gnome of a man with wiry red hair that stood out in all directions on his bulbous skull, he was scowling as he leaned against the gate.

As Cullen and Bitsy stepped up, he pushed away from the rusty metal.

"It's about time you showed up," he said in a raspy voice. "I been here for over an hour waiting for you."

Cullen scowled back at the man as he wrestled with getting the key into the lock. Finally, unable to get the large key to slide into the end of the lock, he stepped aside and let Bitsy try her luck. He turned to Jenkins. "It's only fifteen minutes past our normal opening time, friend," he said. "And, it's not like that old bucket of bolts of yours has somewhere more important to be."

Bitsy easily slipped the key into the lock, turned it, and opened the gate. She walked through, followed by Cullen and the red-faced Jenkins.

"It ain't that I got somewhere important to *be*, it's that I want to get the hell out of this sector as quick as I can."

"You don't like our little planet?" Cullen turned on the man, his large hands balled into fists. At six-four, he towered over the ship owner, who stepped back from him, his narrow face creased in fear.

"Uh, no, it's not like that," he said. "End of the Line's fine as far as backwater planets go. It's just that news I picked up when I dropped cargo off at the Jupiter-3 station indicates that this sector's gonna be a bit unhealthy pretty soon."

Bitsy, who had been walking ahead of them,

stopped at this and turned to face them. "Unhealthy? Mister, I don't know if you noticed, but despite the presence of enough O-2 in the atmosphere to allow breathing unaided, End of the Line has that nasty smell to its air—that comes from the methane farted out by the swamp downwind of the town. I don't see how it could get any unhealthier."

"Aw, little lady," Jenkins said. "If the scuttlebutt I heard be true, this whole sector's about to become a downright dangerous place to be."

"You gonna tell us why," Cullen said. "Or are you just gonna make us guess?"

"Huh? Oh, yeah. What I heard is that some bad critters, called the Grok or Grook—can't recollect which—come in from Gamma Quadrant, and they been attacking the outer settlements. They're heading this way, and whatever the hell they're called, I don't want to be here when they arrive."

"What the hell are Grooks?" Cullen asked.

Jenkins shrank back from Cullen's menacing scowl. "Well, I ain't exactly seen one, but I hear they's near ten feet tall, and they sucks the life out of you and then crushes your bones."

Bitsy laughed. "Sounds like a fairy tale monster to me."

"I don't know nothing about that," Jenkins said. "I do know that four outposts two sectors over no longer answer subspace calls."

"That doesn't mean anything," Cullen said.

"They could just be having interference."

"Maybe, but I heard the Galactic Junkyard was right in the path of these invaders, whatever you call 'em."

Cullen drew himself up to his full height with his fists balled, and glowered down at the little man. "The Galactic what?" There was menace in his voice.

He'd heard the dismissive name before, but never to his face, and it rankled. He didn't remember his grandfather too clearly, other than he liked to drink, yelled a lot whenever he was confused about something, and tended to physical confrontation whenever anyone disagreed with him or upset him, which was often. Cullen didn't yell much, preferring to use a quiet, but menacing voice, but he did like the juju juice that was his grandfather's favorite, and he wasn't averse to fisticuffs whenever he was upset. Anyone who spent longer than a solar day on End of the Line became aware of that. Jenkins seemed to shrink.

"Uh, no insult intended, Mr. Park," he said. "That's just the nickname for this place I heard in the spacer bar over at Helios Prime. I guess it's 'cause you got just about every piece for fixing space ships a body can imagine."

"Lighten up Cullen," Bitsy said. "We *are* a junkyard, so don't get your back up."

Cullen looked at her, his eyes slits. Then, he shrugged and laughed. "Yeah, I guess we are at that."

Jenkins let out a breath. "Say, when will

you have my ship ready to fly?" This he addressed to Bitsy.

She wet an index finger and held it up. "About two hours, three at most."

"Okay, three hours. I'll be back then."

"Be sure you bring payment," Cullen said.

"A hundred kilos of iron, right?"

Cullen nodded. Jenkins blinked, turned, and scurried back toward the Rusty Bucket which had rooms for rent on the second level. Cullen turned to Bitsy. "You sure you can get that thingamajig installed in three hours?"

"Heck, I can get it in in one. I just don't like offworlders bugging me," she said.

"Okay, get it done," he said. "I'll be in my office."

One other trait Cullen had inherited from his grandfather was the practice of taking naps whenever possible rather than strain his body with work. He was a few steps from the door to his office when a shrill voice interrupted him, "Cullen Park, I need to talk to you."

He swore under his breath. He turned slowly, trying to remain expressionless—hard to do considering what he saw approaching him. Moira Nakitomi, proprietor of the Rusty Bucket and governor of End of the Line, was almost as wide as she was tall. Short of thigh and wide of hip, with pendulous breasts that swayed as she bounced along, she had a sneering look on her puffy face.

"Morning, Moira," he said as she came up to him. "What can I do for you?"

TWO

Inside Cullen's office, a small cubbyhole at the back of the repair bay which had an upended engine crate for a desk and four metal oil drums for chairs, Moira Nakitomi sat facing Cullen, her ample buttocks draping over the sides of a drum that seemed barely adequate to hold her body.

Cullen looked across the littered surface of the crate and fought to keep a neutral expression on his face. *Aie-gu, chuketa, no wonder she can only get one man to marry her. She looks like an overweight yakbeast.* He thought of the large, bulbous aquatic animal that was the largest on End of the Line. It looked like an extremely large otter with the face of a whale, and along with the saurofowl, a kind of feathered flying lizard, was the main source of protein for the planet's inhabitants. Moira, he thought, made a yakbeast look svelte, and he was sure it had a more pleasant disposition.

Her evil disposition perfectly matched her appearance and her lineage, too. She looked like the descendant of an escaped desperado—which is what she was. Everyone on End of the Line, in fact, was descended from the original thirty-two colonists—prisoners who were being transported from the Mars colony to a deep space prison station out beyond Pluto. Under the leadership of Tony Park who had been convicted of grand larceny, the prisoners had overpowered their guards, and after doping the guards and ship's crew, and sealing them in escape pods which were programmed to travel to the Luna colony, had taken the prison ship into deep space. They fled until they began running low on fuel, food, and air—just about the time, fortunately, that they spotted M1369X and its two moons. With just enough power to make a landing, they'd opted for the planet instead of the larger moon which contained a rudimentary atmosphere and two large oceans. Now, two generations later, their descendants often gazed up at the night sky, at the small red moon, and the larger blue moon, and wished the coin toss that landed them on the planet which was covered in red dust, black rock, and had only one ocean, which was covered with algae most of the time, had gone the other way.

Despite the fact that she was his cousin, Cullen hated dealing with Moira—hated even being in the same space with her—but, she was in charge, and since his was the major repair facility on the bloody planet, and one of its main sources of revenue, he had no way to avoid her.

"Okay, Moira," he said testily. He had to deal with her, but he didn't have to like it. "What do you want?"

She scowled at him across the makeshift desk. The dislike was entirely mutual. "You could start by being a little more respectful. I am, after all, the designated head of government here."

"Okay, Madam Governor," he said, using her official title. "What can I do for you today?"

"That's better. Look, Cullen, I know you don't like me personally . . . and, I can live with that . . . but, my position is due a certain amount of respect. Anyway, what I came here for . . . well, I need your help."

"As much as I'd like to help you, cou-, er, Madam Governor, you know I'm no good at politics. I'm just a glorified grease monkey."

"Yeah, but you're the only member of the colony who's ever been off world," she said.

He'd once gone to a space station one sector over to help repair a life support system that had malfunctioned. The entire journey had taken three weeks, but, she was right, no one else in End of the Line had ever left the planet's surface since the original settlers crash landed the hijacked prison ship. They remained planet-bound out of ingrained habit. The original settlers never left because they feared being recaptured and sent to serve out their sentences. That habit became a custom, and until Cullen had been asked to go and fix a ship that no one else thought could be repaired, the custom had held. He'd mostly enjoyed seeing different places and different people, although the food and drink, especially the alcoholic drinks, were a bit tepid for his taste.

"What does going off planet have to do with anything?"

"I just got word that F.O.P. is sending a ship, and I need you to deal with them."

"Why would the Federation of Planets send a ship here? We have no resources and our population's too small to support any kind of base," he said.

"I know that, and before you ask, I have no idea why they're sending a ship. All I know is that I don't want to have to deal with them if I don't have to. If you do this for me, I'll owe you big time."

"You think that could extend to lowering my monthly assessment? We haven't had many ships stopping by lately, and the taxes are taking a big bite out of my small stash."

Moira's porcine eyes speared through Cullen. One of her main jobs was collecting monthly assessments from the planet's merchants, and she didn't like not being able to show high receipts. She sighed. Cullen knew from the way she looked like a big balloon that has a pinhole and is slowly leaking, though, that he had her over a barrel, and not just the one she was perched on.

"Okay," she said finally. "I'll knock ten percent off for the next six months. How's that sound?"

"I'd prefer twenty, but I'll take it. When does this ship arrive?"

"Six hours," she said. "I gave them the coordinates of your landing pad."

She hauled her bulk off the barrel and waddled out. Cullen sat watching her leave, thinking how much he'd like to see her staked out on the landing pad when the F.O.P. ship came in for a landing. Then, he remembered that he had a headache, now a dull throbbing.

"I guess I need a bit of the hair of the dog," he mumbled.

He stood and walked gingerly so as not to jostle his tortured brain cells—out of his office, around the side of the building, and toward a large mound of red clay and black rock that stood in the back corner of the compound, just beyond a pile of rusting drive couplings.

In the mound was a door. It was only slightly wider than Cullen's broad shoulders and about an inch higher than his six-foot height. He placed his right thumb over the identification pad. The tiny screen above the pad came to life, blinking yellow, red and green, and finally settling down into a line of green lights. There was a loud clicking sound, and the door swung outward.

He entered a small space, and faced another door which also had a key pad. When the outer door closed, a red light came on over the second door, enabling him to see to put his right thumb over that pad to open the second door, which swung inward with a swooshing sound revealing a large cavern filled with mist. He shivered as he stepped across the sill into the cavern.

To his front, right, and left sat large crates. These contained foodstuffs that had to be kept cool, as well as flagons and bottles of various liquids, the most popular being juju juice. The potent extract made from juju beans had to be kept frigid or it would turn quickly to a bitter liquid with the taste of vinegar and the properties of cleaning fluid.

In addition to repairing the occasional visiting space vessel and other machinery belonging to the colony's residents, he owned the only natural ice chest on End of the Line, which served as the warehouse for perishables, earning him extra credits and ensuring he'd never go broke.

His own stash of perishable items, five crates of juju juice, sat in the very back of the cavern. He went directly to it and opened the nearest crate. From it he extracted six bottles. Tucking them under his arms, he booted the crate closed, and retraced his steps back to the outside.

Back outside in the heat of End of the Line's sun, he took in deep breaths of the hot, dry air. As he started back toward his office, Bitsy came around a stack of engine parts. She was wiping her hands on a greasy rag.

"Hey, Cullen, I—aw, come on . . . you're not diving back into the bottle this early, are you?" Her face wrinkled in disgust.

He gave her a sheepish look. "Uh, actually, I was thinking I'd sort of slide in and wade a little, not dive," he said.

"You've been hitting it really hard lately. What's with you?"

"Nothing," he protested. "I just like my juju juice."

"Whatever." Her look of disgust deepened. "I just wanted to tell you I got that ship done. The captain can pick it up anytime he wants to."

"Sure, why don't you give him a buzz," he said. "He's at the Rusty Bucket." The ground under his feet started vibrating, and a loud roar filled his ears. He clapped his hands over his ears and screwed his eyes up in pain. "Oh, dang, I need a drink fast. The headaches are coming fast and bad."

Bitsy shook her head. "That's not your hangover headache," she said. She pointed upward. "That's a ship coming in to our pad."

He opened his eyes and stared up at the sleek F.O.P. five-man cruiser that was coming down on a column of blue fire, pushing a horrendous wave of sound before it. Leave it to Moira to not even get that right—she'd been wrong about the ship's arrival by six hours.

Charles Ray

THREE

Despite the pain rattling around in his skull, Cullen couldn't help but be impressed with the skill of the cruiser's pilot as he—or she—brought the craft down smoothly in the center of the Park's Parts landing pad.

The main door opened even before the blue vapor from the engines had dissipated. A short, thin man wearing the blue and gray uniform of the Federation of Planets strode down the landing ramp and walked toward Cullen and Bitsy.

As he reached them, he stopped and bowed slightly at the waist. He was a full inch shorter than Bitsy's five-six, and even slighter of build, but he had the expression of a man who made up in bluster what he lacked in bulk. The white letters etched into the black name tag over his left breast read, PISANTE.

"Are you the manager of this

establishment?" he asked, looking at Bitsy.

"No, he is," she said, aiming a thumb at Cullen. "I'm just the grease jockey."

"I'm the *owner*," Cullen said. "What can I do for you, Mr. Pissant?"

"It's PEE-SAHNT, Flight Commander Pisante," the visitor said. "And, your name, sir?"

"Park, Cullen Park," Cullen said. "And, you didn't answer my question. What can I do for you?"

"Yes, of course. We had a radio conversation on the way in with your planetary governor, a Ms. Moira Nakitomi, who said that you were the military liaison for M1369X."

"I'm the wha-, oh, yeah, I guess I am. So what does a fop want here on End of the Line?"

Double circles of red appeared on Pisante's sallow cheeks. The look he gave Cullen was withering. He took a deep breath before speaking.

"Is there somewhere we could discuss business . . . in *private*?" He looked pointedly at Bitsy.

Cullen smiled. "Ms. Jacobs is my associate," he said. "I have no secrets from her."

Pisante looked uncomfortable. He shrugged. "Very well, Mr. Park, if you insist. May we retire to your office?"

"Sure, follow me."

Pisante turned toward his ship. A tall, gaunt officer dressed in the same blue and gray uniform stood at the top of the ramp. "Mr. Frank," he said. "Would you please join us?" He turned back to Cullen and Bitsy. "Lieutenant Frank is my executive officer. He'll be taking notes of our meeting."

"It'll be a little crowded in my office," Cullen said. "And, I only have . . . four . . . chairs."

"Mr. Frank won't mind standing," Pisante said.

"Suit yourself." Cullen shrugged and kept walking.

Once inside his office, he took the barrel behind his crate desk. Bitsy sat on the one in front of the crate. Cullen pointed at two other barrels in the corner. Pisante's face darkened, but he grabbed one of the rusty containers and rocked and rolled it into position beside Cullen. He had to do a little skip to get himself up and onto it. Frank stepped inside the door, took one look at the remaining barrel, and leaned back against the wall. He took out an electro-steno pad, holding it up at chest level.

Pisante wriggled his skinny buttocks to find a comfortable position atop the barrel. After he brushed the wrinkles out of his pants legs, he looked at Cullen, whose face was still above his.

"Now, Mr. Park," he said. "Here's our situation. An aggressive race from the Omega Quadrant, known as the G'rok, is invading our solar system. They've already taken several of the outlying planets and deep space stations. We have it on good authority that their current line of advance will bring them through this sector . . . in fact, it's likely that M1369X—or as you people call it, End of the Line—is on their list of targets."

Cullen and Bitsy shared a look.

"Why would aliens want to invade us?" Bitsy asked.

Pisante ignored, directing his remarks at Cullen.

"We still don't know a lot about the G'rok, and frankly, their motives are irrelevant . . . intelligence indicates they're heading this way."

"So, what the hell are we supposed to do about it?" Cullen found the man's demeanor irritating. "We have no weapons to fight them, so I guess if they show up, we'll just have to surrender."

"That, Mr. Cullen, is *not* an option," Pisante said. "The Federation has decided that the G'rok must not go beyond this point. We're to hold the line here."

Cullen looked at the man as if he'd just changed into a yakbeast. Not only was he arrogant, he was looney.

"Look around you, Mr., uh . . . Flight Commander Pisante. Did you see any fighters or cruisers when you came out of subspace? Other than that little pea shooter you're riding in, do you see anything that could fight off a space scout troop, much less a bunch of invading aliens?"

"I have a battleship and six destroyers six to eight hours behind me," Pisante said. "We plan to meet and defeat the G'rok right here on . . . End of the Line." He chuckled. "A rustic name for a planet, but quite appropriate actually."

FOUR

"My plan," Pisante said, puffing out his chest like a male saurofowl. "Is to hide the battleship and two destroyers behind Europa, your larger Moon, and the remaining four destroyers behind Calisto, the smaller, and when the G'rok approach M1369X, to ambush and destroy them." As he spoke, his eyes blinked rapidly, and he looked at a spot on the wall behind Cullen.

Cullen was no military genius—hc'd only ever met one military person before, a young recruit he'd met in a bar the one time he'd been off world—but, it occurred to him that anyone planning to invade End of the Line might send scouts ahead to get the lay of the land, so to speak, and those scouts were very likely to spot seven large, heavily armed space ships lurking behind the planet's moons. He noticed that Lieutenant Frank had a skeptical look on his face as his commander talked.

"Uh, I've never been in the military, and I don't know much about how you do things," Cullen said. "But, isn't that a dangerous thing to do? I mean, what if these Groks send scouts, and they spot your guys hiding up there behind the moons?"

Pisante tilted his head back, regarding Cullen icily down the length of his nose.

"You are correct, Mr. Park," he said. "You don't know much about how we do things. I assure you, this is a perfectly good plan. Why, it's similar to a plan I came up with during an exercise at the academy. Caught the opposition flat footed, it did. I got the highest marks in my tactics class. And, it's not Grok, by the way, it's G'rok"

Cullen had never been to a fancy school either, but he wanted to say that things in the real world didn't often work out the way they do in classrooms. Somehow, though, he didn't think Pisante would appreciate the observation. On the other hand, there was still what might happen to him and his fellow citizens if these 'whatever you called them' aliens discovered that End of the Line was an ambush. They might blame the citizens of the planet and take it out on them.

"Okay, so you're the tactical expert," he said. "I'm willing to concede that. But, what happens if they *do* spot your ambush? We're not exactly fortified against an ambush from space, you know. Jupiter, we can't handle an attack from anywhere."

"They won't spot it," Pisante said. "And, even if they do, I'm sure we can match them in firepower. My forces should make short work of them."

That didn't make Cullen feel one bit better actually. He really disliked Moira at this point for placing him in this situation. Military liaison, indeed. From the pained look on Frank's face, he was beginning to think Pisante was a paper soldier—someone who'd done very well in school, but had never actually put anything he'd learned into practice—and, that couldn't be good for End of the Line. In fact, it could be the end of the line for End of the Line.

"If you outnumber these Gr-, er, aliens, why don't you meet them somewhere in deep space and wipe them out, rather than letting them break out of subspace over a planet where civilian lives are put at risk?"

Pisante's face darkened, and his tiny eyes blinked rapidly. "Well, er, you see . . . we don't know their exact course or position at the moment . . . and, we only have an estimate of the size of their armada. We're still . . . trying to . . . get a fix on them."

"Don't you know *anything* about them?" Bitsy asked.

Cullen shot her a smile. She winked at him. Pisante made a gargling sound in his throat. Frank put a hand over his mouth to conceal a smile.

Pisante gave Bitsy a withering look. She gazed back at him with her big blue eyes, a perfectly innocent look on her face. Cullen had to fight the urge to laugh. He'd seen Bitsy do this before—looking all naïve and innocent, just before she skewered some sucker to the wall.

"We actually know a lot about them," Pisante said, looking directly at her for the first time as he spoke. "We know, for instance, that they're not mammalian as we humans are. They're a reptilian, bipedal species that arose on some of the watery planets of their system. They've reportedly stripped most of their own planets of the resources they require to survive, and are now seeking new planets to plunder."

"Well, I don't understand why they'd want to invade us," Cullen said. "We have a little water, but precious little else."

"If I may, sir," Frank said, stepping away from the wall. "I think I can answer that question."

Pisante frowned at his subordinate, but waved him to go on.

"Our intel folks think the G'rok want to use End of the Line as a staging base for the takeover of the entire system," he continued.

Cullen smiled at the man's use of the local name rather than the designation in the atlas.

"Why would they want to do that? We're in the middle of nowhere," he said. "About the only advantage we have is that we're near the sector border, so it's convenient for ships to get repairs . . . oh, I see."

"That's right," Frank said. "A base here is far from our bases, but close to the border. If they established themselves here, it would be difficult for us to root them out, but they'd be somewhat centrally located between their home planets and their targets. If we hadn't picked up on this information after their last attack on Goren base, they might have been able to set up right under our noses."

"Well," Bitsy said. "Not exactly under your noses. Some of the spacers who visit here say we're located in another part of the galaxy's anatomy—it's nether regions, I understand?"

Frank laughed. He cut his laughter short after Pisante shot him a withering glare.

"Well put, Miss," Frank said. "But, that is also not a part of the anatomy you want the bad guys to be set up."

"Yeah, I guess that could be a real pain in the backside," Cullen said. "So, what do you fops plan to do about it?"

Frank snickered again, and Pisante glared. Bitsy laughed out loud.

"The *Federation of Planets* plans to establish a base here on M1369X," Pisante said. "That base will be a barrier to further G'rok encroachment." Again his eyes flickered, only this time he looked at the floor.

Bitsy raised her hand, sending a questioning look at Cullen.

"Yes, Bit-, er, Miss Jacobs?" he said.

"It's been a while since I was in school," she said. Actually, she'd just finished twelfth grade, the highest education available on End of the Line, two years earlier. "But, I do seem to recall that a vote by the planetary parliament is required before F.O.P. can set up any kind of installation."

Frank nodded. "That's true, Miss Jacobs."

Pisante glared pure hatred at him. Cullen gave Pisante his best innocent look. It wasn't as good as Bitsy's, but he was proud of it.

"So . . . Flight Commander *Pisante,*" Cullen said. "Did you get a vote approving establishment of a base?"

He, of course, knew the answer to that question. End of the Line's legislative body, more like a city council, consisted of five people, chaired by Moira Nakitomi, and if she'd known about a base, and the council had approved it, despite her dislike of Cullen, she would have informed him. He wasn't surprised, therefore, at the way Pisante's face drooped sadly, or the way he shook his head.

"Uh, no," he said. "I assumed that as the military liaison, you would have the requisite authority to grant basing rights."

Cullen smiled wolfishly. "No, I'm afraid I don't have that authority. I guess I'll have to consult with the council and get back to you."

"And, how long will that take?" Pisante had a look of disbelief on his face. He was apparently not accustomed to being on the receiving end of bureaucracy.

"Well," Cullen said. "I have to walk into town. Then, I have to find the governor, and she'll have to call the council members. Oh, I'd say two . . . three hours at least."

"We don't have a lot of time. We need to make some decisions before the arrival of . . . my ships. I need to be able to give them their final orders."

"I'll head to town lickety-split. You're welcome to stay here if you want. Bitsy'll see to you."

Frank smiled, but Pisante looked around Cullen's tiny office and made a face as if someone had loosed a silent but deadly fart. "No, that's fine," he said. "We'll wait in the ship."

Charles Ray

FIVE

It took Cullen a mere fifteen minutes to walk from his shop to the Rusty Bucket. When he delivered Pisante's message to Moira, she got on the land line and called the other council members to an emergency session. In twenty minutes more, seven people sat around a large round table in the now-closed to business Rusty Bucket. Moira rapped the top of the table with a large spoon to bring the meeting to order.

A round table doesn't have a head or a hierarchical order of seating, but somehow, by the way she arranged things, with her back to the bar in the back of the room and with Cullen seated at her left side, Moira appeared to be at the head of the table.

To her right was the deputy governor, Helen Hajib, who also was the owner and operator of End of the Line's only hotel. Next to her was Larry Jackson, president of the Farmers'

Association and owner of the largest guggle melon farm on the planet. Next to him sat Sandra Little Elk, her bronze face impassive and framed by jet black hair, she wore a dress that she'd woven herself, befitting her status as the owner of the only clothing manufacturing facility. She was also the colony's historian, not that anyone besides here as particularly interested in history, but it did help when people wanted to confirm parentage before getting married. Patrick Gonzales, whose father had first domesticated yakbeasts, ran the planet's meat processing facility. Finally, sitting between him and Cullen was Melanie Chang, the planet's librarian, and proprietor of House of Delights, which continued in the tradition of her grandmother, Jade Sung, who had been convicted in a Mars colony court for murdering and robbing patrons of the house of pleasure she ran there. Upon landing on End of the Line, Jade had set up shop, for everyone except the three men she took as her husbands, and as the population grew and spacers began to discover the out of the way backwater, had prospered. She'd passed House of Delights to her daughter, Lorelei Chang, who had expanded it before passing it to Melanie.

A large pot of coffee, ringed with white porcelain cups, sat in the center of the table. After everyone had poured a cup, Moira tapped an empty cup she kept near her left elbow. The spoon she used made a ringing sound.

"Ladies and gentlemen, you will please come

to order," she said.

"What's so important that you had to call an emergency meeting?" Helen Hajib asked in her high-pitched, whiny voice.

"Yeah, I'm right in the middle of harvesting my melon crop," Jackson said. "I really don't like leaving my workers unsupervised."

Moira looked at Cullen. "Cullen here has some news for us," she said. "Cullen, why don't you tell everyone what your friend from F.O.P. wants to do?"

Cullen gulped his coffee, giving Moira a dirty look as he wiped his chin with the sleeve of his tunic. "I wouldn't exactly call Flight Commander Pisante a friend," he said.

"Did you say Pissant?" Patrick Gonzales asked.

"No, although he is something of a piss ant, he prefers to be called PeeSahnt," Cullen said, smiling. "Anyway, what he wants is to set up a Federation military base here on End of the Line, and he needs your approval as the planctary government."

"Why, after all these years of ignoring us, do the fops suddenly want to plunk a bunch of soldiers down in our midst?" Sandra Little Elk held her coffee cup in front of her mouth as she spoke.

Cullen smiled. Leave it to her to get straight to the point.

"They think some aliens called Gr . . . G'roks . . . are heading this way and plan to invade us," he said.

Jackson's mouth dropped open. "Uh, invade, as in shooting up the place invade?"

"That's what they said," Cullen said. "A freighter captain said the same thing earlier, too. Apparently these G'rok are some kind of lizards who like to take over and pillage planets, and they been making their way in from the edge of the system for a while now."

"Good guggle melon," Jackson said. "We're in no shape to deal with an invasion."

"Unless we had a squadron of fop soldiers here to defend us," Hajib said.

"That would put quite a strain on our resources, though," Moira said. "Where would we put so many people?"

"Well," Hajib said. "My hotel is more than half empty, and if the military plans to be here permanently, I could expand."

"My girls and I could definitely use the extra business," Melanie Chang said. "Spacer traffic has been pretty light lately."

Moira laid a pudgy finger against her nose. "I see your point. I suppose my place could use the extra customers as well."

"Yes, but is it worth the aggravation?" Sandra Little Elk's face creased with worry. "Once the Federation plants roots, it's like a scratchvine; it starves out other plants, is prickly as hell, and is impossible to get rid of."

Cullen could sympathize with her view. His one trip off world, even though enjoyable, had left him with a sour view of the people of other planets, especially the bureaucrats of the

Federation of Planets, a bunch of self-righteous prigs who thought themselves above everyone else. He'd seen the way they dealt with the common citizens of the town he'd visited. Their high-handedness would not go down well on End of the Line.

Moira Nakitomi, on the other hand, was looking around the table at her fellow council members. Cullen could tell she was trying to assess which way the majority was going.

"You might be right, Sandra," she said. "But, if we're about to be invaded, we might need the Federation to survive."

"How do we know for sure these lizards are planning to invade us?" Gonzales asked.

"Where the hell we gonna put their ships, where will they be housed?" Jackson asked. He looked at Hajib. "You can't house that many people in that hotel of yours, and if you expand, that'll mean taking land away from farming and ranching."

"It will also upset the social order," Little Elk addcd.

It appeared to Cullen that things were breaking down into a deadlock. The merchants on the council in favor of the Federation presence, while the land owners and the sole historian were against it. He wondered how Moira would deal with it.

She answered his question by turning and staring at him. "I think," she said. "That our new military liaison is perhaps in the best position to help us decide."

"Huh, hey, I'm not part of the council," Cullen said. "I don't have any part in the decisions you guys make."

Moira smiled. "Good point, Cullen," she said. "Ladies and gentlemen of the Council, I propose that Cullen Park be appointed Council Military Liaison, and be given full responsibility to deal with the Federation of Planets military forces and to work with them to defend End of the Line against a possible invasion. All in favor please raise your right hand." Six hands went up. "I see no objections. So moved. Cullen, you are now the official military liaison for End of the Line, and as such, you're designated the authority to make the decisions related to the position."

"Hey," Cullen said. "You can't do that." He wasn't actually sure what the council could legally do. He'd spent most of his life avoiding it. "I didn't apply for this job."

"But, Cullen, my dear cousin, we can," Moira said. Her voice was as sweet and sticky as treacle. "Since you've told us we're about to be invaded, that makes this an emergency—oh, and this *is* an emergency meeting—and, in an emergency, the council can make emergency appointments, and those appointed are required to serve or be banished from the colony. That was one of the first rules our founders made when they landed here, right Sandra?" Little Elk nodded.

He knew that she was right. A bunch of escaped prisoners would have required some pretty draconian rules to ensure their cooperation in the early days of the settlement. And, it sounded like something his grandfather Tony Park would come up with. If Sandra Little Elk said it was so, he had no choice but to believe it. The woman never lied. As much as he hated the idea of being squeezed into the corner, a glance around the table showed him that Moira's move met with everyone's approval. He would have to make the best of it.

"Okay . . . just so you know, I really don't want the job," he said. "But, I'll do my best."

"Are you planning to let the F.O.P. establish a base?" Chang asked. She had a hopeful expression on her face, and her almond-shaped eyes gleamed.

"You're not, are you?" Jackson's expression was not hopeful, and his eyes didn't gleam.

Cullen felt more squeezed into a corner. No matter what decision he made, he felt that he would have people mad at him. What, he thought, would Grandpa Park do in a situation like this? Then, it hit him. His grandfather would avoid making a decision for as long as he could.

"I'll have to get more information from this guy Pisante before I can make up my mind," he said. "I'll be sure to let the council know when I do."

Before they could question him further, he stood and beat a hasty retreat.

Charles Ray

SIX

When Cullen got back to the repair shop, he found Bitsy sitting in his office deep in conversation with Lieutenant Frank. They both looked up sheepishly when he entered. Bitsy's cheeks flamed red.

"So . . . how did your meeting with the council go?" she asked. "Did they approve F.O.P. stationing troops here?"

Cullen affected not noticing the embarrassed looks on their faces, but inside he was laughing. Bitsy had never shown interest in the opposite gender before, preferring to spend her time up to her elbows in a spaceship's engines, so he was happy that she'd finally learned that she was a girl—and a quite good looking girl at that.

"Not exactly," he said. He then explained how Moira's assignment of him to be military liaison so she could avoid dealing with the visitors had turned into an official, council-approved position. "I am now the official Military Liaison Officer for End of the Line."

"What does that mean, exactly?" Frank asked.

"It means they've passed the buck to me to determine what to do about you fellows and these G'rok, who you say are hell bent on invading us."

"Well, what are you going to do about it? Morley . . . uh, Lieutenant Frank needs to know," Bitsy said.

"I thought Pisante was in charge."

"Uh, he is," Frank said. "But, as his exec, I'm responsible for developing tactical plans, feeding and housing the troops . . . just about everything but making the big strategic and tactical decisions."

"In other words," Cullen said. "You do the work and Pissant, er, Pisante, gets the credit."

"You talk like someone who has spent time in the military."

Cullen laughed. "No, I've only been off planet once in my life, but dealing with people like Pisante isn't all that different from dealing with politicians like our governor. You and I seem to have been put in the same leaky escape pod, and I don't have an astromap . . . what about you? What have you got, Lieutenant Frank?"

The Federation of Planets officer looked intently at Cullen. As they locked gazes, Cullen could see that the man was troubled. He seemed to be wrestling with some momentous decision. As the muscles of his jaw relaxed, Cullen felt that he'd come to a decision.

"For starters," Frank said. "Just call me Morley. And, as to what I have . . . well, not much other than a bit of corrected information that you need to know before you make any decision."

As the descendant of a con man, Cullen wasn't surprised at much that people did. He thought maybe Pisante had fed him false information about an invasion—for what reason, though, he could not fathom. "There's no invasion?" he asked hopefully.

"Oh, there'll be an invasion all right enough," Frank said. "The timing of things, though, isn't quite what the flight commander told you."

Cullen walked behind his 'desk' and sat on the edge of the barrel. He looked across at Frank. "Okay," he said. "Let me have it."

"Well, for starters, our forces are more like twenty hours behind us, and the intelligence we have indicates that it's the G'rok who will be here in six to eight hours – well, more like four to five hours now—and, that's just a guess on my part."

Cullen felt as if he'd been kicked in the gut by a yakbeast. An alien invasion in four to five hours and the only help more than twenty hours away.

"Holy crud," he said. "What are we supposed

to do? We can't deal with an alien armada."

Frank took a deep breath. "Look, I'm going to tell you something, but you have to promise—both of you—never to tell another living soul. I could end up in a penal colony for the rest of my life if it got out."

Bitsy laid a hand on his arm and smiled warmly at him. "You know I'd never tell, Morley," she said. Cullen had never heard such warmth in her voice.

"Sure," he said. "Mum's the word."

"Okay, here it is. Flight Commander Pisante never had any intention of hiding our fleet and ambushing the G'rok. He knew the G'rok would get here before our people and would easily take the planet. His plan was to get your okay for a Federation base on the planet, and then after our forces attacked and defeated the G'rok, we could come in afterwards and set up the base. It's all part of a plan to expand our military presence in this part of the sector."

Cullen felt his cheeks burn with anger. Damn bureaucrats, whether they were military or political, they were all the same, forever trying to manipulate others.

"Why in Jupiter didn't he just tell me that from the start?"

"A lot of the smaller settlements don't want a military presence on their planets," Frank said. "It's an administrative burden, and it tends to restrict some of the freedoms the outlying settlements have come to take for granted. My guess is he didn't want to take a chance on being turned down. I mean, if we come after you've been invaded, even though we defeat the enemy, there's the risk that your council won't want us here."

"Well," Cullen said. "He's not far wrong there. At least half the council opposes it. The ones that do are only interested in the money they might make from your presence. I have a feeling that once you're here, even they'll have second thoughts. I suppose, though, the commander won't be too anxious to defend us if I deny his request?"

"I can't really say." Frank shrugged. "It is our duty to defeat the G'rok and keep them from taking over Federation space. Of course, he could let you people suffer, and decided to attack the G'rok on some other planet."

"In that case, I'll just have to not turn him down."

"So, you'll approve a base?"

Cullen smiled. "I didn't say that. I said I won't turn him down. I need time to mull this over. He's a burcaucrat. He won't like it, but he can't argue with it. In the meantime, we need to figure out what we're going to do about the G'rok."

Charles Ray

SEVEN

Five hundred thousand kilometers from End of the Line, in a remote sector of space, five large bulbous green ships streaked silently through the blackness. They were silent only because space is mostly vacuum, and there's nothing in a vacuum to carry sound.

The flagship, in the middle of the five-ship formation, was the largest of them all. On the flight deck, encased in battle armor, and seated in a large command chair, the commander of the flotilla stared at the wide navigation screen that took up most of the front wall. He tapped a gloved appendage on the arm of the chair and made hissing sounds over his com unit. The armor-clad crew members hunched over their stations, and tried to make themselves as small as possible. No one wanted to draw Supreme Broodmaster K'rket's attention.

"What is the time of our arrival at the target," K'rket's oily, sibilant voice said over the general com channel to no one in particular.

The navigation officer quivered. It was her job to know, and therefore, it must be her to respond, knowing that if he was displeased by her response, punishment would be swift and severe.

"Two standard ticks, Supreme Broodmaster," she said. She fought to keep a quaver out of her voice. That would be a sign of weakness, which, if it didn't cause K'rket to flay her with his neural whip, would invite others in the crew to attack. Such was the way the social order of the G'rok operated.

It must have worked. She didn't feel the sting of the whip, and a few furtive glances informed her that none of her crew mates were poised to attack.

"Very well, then," K'rket said. "Weapons Officer, make sure your stations are ready."

The weapons officer, two stations down from navigation, snapped to attention. "All is in readiness, Supreme Broodmaster," he said.

Standing next to K'rket, First Officer L'tel, made a clicking sound in his throat, the sign a low born used to get the attention of a member of the G'rok royal family, for K'rket was one thousandth in line for the throne of the G'rok Empire.

"Speak, L'tel," K'rket said, and waved his

right appendage in the air.

"I am most grateful for the chance to speak, Most Honorable Supreme Broodmaster," L'tel said. "I have an interrogative."

"What is it, fool?" Sometimes K'rket was frustrated by the interminable formalities required for a low born member of his crew to initiate a conversation. He would never utter such thoughts aloud, in particular would he not say such things in the presence of either lowborns or members of his own social status, but he found the structure of G'rok society very inefficient. If he ever became emperor he would give serious consideration to modifying it to allow freer interchange of information. The current structure impeded the development of ideas, and the lack of new ideas was the reason the G'rok Empire was currently suffering.

"Does the Supreme Broodmaster think the warm blooded ones will have forces to meet us at the target?"

"Have they met us with force at any other placc?" K'rket raised himself from the chair and stared down at his second in command through the anti-glare goggles he wore over his face. "No, I do not expect them to meet us with force. In fact, I expect them to do what every other brood of these creatures has done—to surrender immediately. Once they see how impressive and implacable we are, what choice do they have?"

"Will the Supreme Broodmaster be going down to the surface to take their surrender?"

"Yes, Executive Officer L'tel," he said. "I will

be going to the surface to take their surrender."

"How many soldiers will you take with you, Supreme Broodmaster?"

K'rket considered the question for ten beats of his two hearts. The routine was boring. L'tel had done it just before each operation, as it was dictated by his instructions, and the poor fool had no choice but to follow his instructions. Sometimes, K'rket wished someone on his vessel would vary from instructions, so that he would have an excuse to use his neural whip. Not that he really needed an excuse, but he didn't want to get a reputation as being one of those flighty royals who punished on a mere whim. He considered himself a professional military officer, and tried to conduct himself with the proper decorum at all times. He knew that once this campaign was finished, the jockeying to move up in the line of succession would begin, and a stellar military record would help him immeasurably. So, he reasoned, would a record of bravery.

"I think, Executive Officer L'tel, that two soldiers to escort me should be sufficient. I leave it to you to choose the two who will accompany me."

L'tel bowed stiffly at the waist. "It will be as you wish, Supreme Broodmaster."

Silently, he withdrew to comply with his orders, leaving K'rket to contemplate the slightly less than two ticks until they came into the gravitational pull of the ball of rock, dust, and water that he'd been watching on his screens for the past two cycles.

Although he would never say it in front of any of the low born who crewed the vessels in his flotilla, he thought the whole campaign was a colossal waste of time and that his time and talents would be better spent in other pursuits. But, Emperor K'gal, his uncle or cousin—he was never quite sure—had decided, and the emperor's word was law on G'rok. To disobey meant exile to one of the prison compounds on the moon at best, instant execution at worst. Actually, he thought, instant execution was probably the preferred punishment, since royals didn't tend to live too long in the prison compounds. Once the low born prisoners identified them, they tended to kill them slowly and painfully. There'd never been a report of the guards at any of the facilities intervening to save the life of an imprisoned member of the royal family. So, even though he thought he was on a fool's errand, he would say nothing. He would execute his duties to the best of his ability, so K'gal would have no excuse to execute him.

K'rket fancied himself more scientist than military, and he was convinced that it was science that had the answer to G'rok's current problem, not military action.

True, the home world, as well as the other planets of the system, was suffering a decline in essential resources, but the levels hadn't quite reached a point where there was not enough for the population. Proper application of scientific methods could increase production. Taking over new worlds was, he was convinced, was *not* the answer. It was, in fact, merely postponing the inevitable unless they started taking actions to conserve resources. And, he feared, with the additional planets in the inventory, future crises would be even more severe.

He could not, of course, say such a thing to K'gal and his council of ministers. Senile old reptiles one and all, accustomed to unconditional obedience to their every whim. So, he would go on, taking planets, enslaving their populations, and establishing settlements for the immigrants from G'rok's home world who would soon arrive. At least, he thought, it would mean a slightly less population density on the home world, so it wasn't a total loss.

The navigator made the clicking noise.

"Speak," K'rket said.

"Supreme Broodmaster," the navigator said. "We are about to enter orbit around the planet known by the warm blooded ones as M1369X."

EIGHT

Cullen pointed to the chronometer on his office wall.

"Flight Commander Pisante," he said. "You will notice that six hours have gone by since you arrived. You mind telling me why we haven't heard from the Federation ships you said would arrive? Even if they were eight hours away, they should be calling by now to announce their arrival."

Pisante refused to make eye contact. Like a misbehaving student who has been called to the headmaster's office, he sat on the barrel looking down at his highly polished boots which, because of his lack of stature, didn't quite reach the floor.

"Uh, these things can't always be estimated with pinpoint accuracy," he said. "They're probably just a little behind schedule."

If Cullen had been his grandfather, this is the point where he would have started sputtering and screaming obscenities. While he had inherited his grandpa's temper, he'd learned self-control from his father. Jubilee had only inherited the broad brow, sleek black hair, and almond eyes from the Korean side of his family. From his mother, Zainab Kamara, a forger whose ancestors had originally come from the West African region on the planet earth, he had inherited smooth skin the color of caramel, and a placid disposition. Cullen's skin was like caramel with a dollop of milk, but as smooth as his father's had been, and even though it upset his stomach at times, he was able to keep his temper mostly in check. Looking at Pisante squirming atop the barrel, he had to work extra hard to keep from spitting invective at the man.

"I suppose you're right," he said after taking a few breaths to center himself. "But, could there be another explanation?"

"Maybe, but I doubt it. I mean . . . if they'd encountered the G'rok . . . well, I would have been informed."

Cullen laughed, but there was no mirth in it. "That's not what I mean," he said. He stood and looked down at Pisante. He was momentarily distracted by the glint of light off the top of the man's skull where the hair was thinning and showing a lot of pink. "What I mean, is I don't think your ships were due here when you said they were due."

"W-what do you mean?" Pisante's cheeks turned red. "Are you implying that I, an officer of the Federation of Planets Interstellar Defense Force, am being less than truthful?"

Cullen could feel his grandfather's genes screaming inside his skull. He could imagine what Tony Park would be doing right now. He'd be spitting mad. In fact, he'd be literally spitting as he hurled harsh invective across the rickety desk at the scrawny little bureaucrat perched atop the rusty barrel. Of course, if Jubilee was there, he'd be saying, "Don't lose your temper, son. When you lose your temper, you lose control of the situation." That's what his father would say. His mother, Annabel O'Grady, a fiery redhead who was the daughter of Cynthia Miller, a murderer, and Seam O'Grady, a smuggler, would pat Jubilee fondly on the head and turning to Cullen, say, "Your father's right Cullen. Don't lose your temper. Just quietly take this vermin by the throat and slowly shake him to death."

His parents had taught him the middle way—cold vengeance.

"No, *Mr. Pissant*, I'm not implying that you're being less than truthful," he said. "I'm *saying* that you're blowing yakbeast manure into my breathing mask, and it stinks."

Pisante's face went bright red. His eyes goggled, and his mouth flew open. He had probably never been spoken to in that manner since putting on the uniform, and certainly not by a civilian. He drew himself up as high as he could manage without toppling from the barrel, still having to look up at Cullen who was now standing with his hands on his hips and scowling down at him.

"The name, sir, is Pisante," he said. "And, I'd appreciate it if you'd quit butchering it. And, I'm an officer in the IDF. You will address me as Flight Commander Pisante."

"I wasn't saying your name," Cullen said. "I was describing you. Okay, flight commander, if that's the way you want it. But, I'm getting a bit fed up with the crap you're feeding me. We save it for the guggle melon fields."

"I don't understand what you mean, sir."

"I mean," Cullen said slowly as if speaking to a slightly backwards child. "That you need to stop telling me lies. This might be a backwater planet, and we might not be as sophisticated as the people on Mars and Luna Base, but we're not fools. I know the fleet you promised in six to eight hours is probably twice as far away as you said, and that it's likely these G'rok will get here first. Tell me I got it wrong."

Beads of sweat popped out on Pisante's forehead. He looked as if he was about to hyperventilate. This was not the way it was supposed to be. The hicks on this backwater planet were just supposed to be happy the

IDF was on the scene and agree to whatever he proposed. They certainly weren't supposed to be perceptive enough to see through the fiction that a fleet of IDF warships were only hours behind him. Even worse, the oaf looked as if he wanted to slam his fist into something—like Pisante's face. The situation was delicate, and would require all of his skill to manage.

"Uh, well, no you're not exactly wrong," he said. "The IDF ships are about twelve to sixteen hours away. Frankly, we don't know how far away the G'rok ships are. Intelligence indicates that they've taken two planets at the border of the sector, but all radio contact was lost shortly after they arrived, so we can only guess about their present position."

"So, how do you even know they're heading this way?"

"Our analysts looked at the line of their conquests and projected that they'd come this way," Pisante said. "Your little planet is a bit off the beaten path only as far as commercial trade routes are concerned. It happens to be located ideally, however, as a base from which to launch ships, and it's almost halfway between Earth and where we estimate the G'rok home world to be."

Cullen did some fast figuring. Anyone wishing to travel to either of the two home worlds would have an advantage basing on End of the Line. Cullen's home had now become the center of the line—for the G'roks at least. It didn't explain why the earth forces wanted a base there, though . . . unless-, "You wouldn't happen to be planning to invade the G'rok planets, would you?"

Pisante's red face suddenly paled. Cullen smiled inwardly. He'd hit the stress bolt on the head.

"You are," he continued. "You're planning to invade G'rok, and you want to use End of the Line as your launch base. Once the G'rok learn that, we'd be the main aim of their forces. This planet would become a battleground."

Pisante's Adam's apple bobbed up and down. "W-well, there's always the possibility of extended combat in this region," he said. "We might have to relocate the population of the planet."

"Wha-, stop your engines, mister," Cullen said. "Ain't nobody from here going anywhere. The way I see it, if you don't have a base here, the G'rok won't have a reason to invade."

"D-does that mean you're denying my request to establish an IDF base?"

As angry at the man as he was, Cullen wasn't quite ready to burn that bridge. He wanted his home protected. What he didn't want, or particularly like, was that Pisante seemed intent on uprooting him from that home. What he needed to do was keep his options open.

"No, flight commander, I'm not denying

your request. I'm just not approving it yet. I need to think on it more."

Pisante's mouth opened and closed. He regarded Cullen through half-closed lids. Cullen looked back at him, a placid expression on his brown face. Finally, Pisante shrugged, jumped off the barrel and stalked out of the office.

Charles Ray

NINE

Seconds after Pisante's departure, Bitsy came in. She had a worried look on her face.

"Pisante looked a bit angry just now," she said. "What did you say to him?"

"Well, I called him a liar."

"That would make me angry."

"What really upset him, though, is I didn't approve him setting up a military base here."

"You turned him down?"

Cullen laughed. "No, I just didn't approve his request."

"You-, oh, I see," she said, laughing. "I guess that would upset him. What are we going to do, though, about this invasion?"

He hadn't thought it through that far. He didn't want to have himself or his friends uprooted, but he didn't want them killed either.

"I'm still thinking on that, too," he said. "It would help, I suppose, if we knew more about these aliens. You think your friend Morley would help us?"

Her cheeks darkened. "He's not my friend," she said. "We were just-"

He waved a hand at her. "It doesn't matter, Bitsy. It's clear he likes you. Maybe you could invite him in for a drink . . . and we could have a little chat."

"Really, you think he likes me?"

Cullen wanted to laugh. If the situation hadn't been so desperate, he would have. He'd never seen Bitsy act this way before.

"Yeah, Bitsy, I think he likes you."

What was there not to like. Even with grease smudges on her face, she was the prettiest girl on End of the Line. Actually, Cullen was beginning to wonder why he'd never noticed it before.

"Okay, I guess I could ask him," she said.

She left, and returned a few minutes later. Morley Frank followed close behind her. He had a loopy smile on his face, which turned to a puzzled frown when he saw Cullen.

"Uh, Mr. Park, I didn't know you were here."

Cullen pointed at the barrel recently vacated by Pisante. "Have a seat, Morley," he said. "We need to talk. Would you like a drink of juju juice?"

"Yeah, I guess I'm off duty now. What do you want to talk about?"

Cullen took a bottle of juju juice from the

shelf behind his desk and three dusty tin cups. He blew off the dust and filled them. One he passed to Frank, another to Bitsy, and took a sip from the third. The stuff had been in the shelf for a few hours, and would have to be consumed soon or it would turn sour.

He put his cup down. "It's like this, Morley," he said. "We need to know everything you can tell us about these G'rok."

Frank took a tentative sip of the juju juice. His face turned red and his eyes got as round as small saucers. "H-holy Jupiter," he said, gasping. "W-what is this stuff?"

Bitsy took a long swallow and wiped her lips with her sleeve. "This, Morley, my dear, is the juice of the juju berry. You don't like it?"

He swallowed, took another sip, and fought to keep it going down. A third sip went down easier. "Uh, it's like nothing I've ever drunk before," he said. "We don't have anything this strong on any of the other worlds I've been on . . . certainly not in the IDF canteens." He took a fourth sip, smiling as it slid easily down his throat. "It's actually pretty good. Kind of grows on you."

"Yeah," Cullen said, knocking back half of what was in his cup. "It'll grow hair on your tongue if you're not careful. Can't keep it in your mouth too long or it'll take the enamel off your teeth. Now, let's get down to business. What can you tell us about the

G'rok?"

Frank emptied his cup and held it out for a refill. "Okay, but you have to give me more of this stuff."

"Hey, go easy. You drink too much of this and you won't be able to talk."

He poured the cup half full. Frank took a sip.

"All right, here's the deal," he said. "The G'rok are a species that was descended from the lizards . . . animals sort of like the dinosaurs back on Earth. They evolved as the dominant species on their home world, discovered space flight around the same time our species was discovering it back on old Earth."

He took another sip.

"Say, this is really good. Can I get a few bottles to take with me when we leave?" Cullen smiled acknowledgement. "Okay, where was I? Oh yeah, so the G'rok have this patriarchal social system, with a hereditary monarch . . . an emperor. The royal lines hold most of the leadership positions, while the lower classes do the work. Not unlike humans, they have a tendency to abuse their environment. We've heard, although it hasn't been confirmed, that they've exhausted most of the food resources on their home planet and the other habitable planets in their system, so they've busted out to find other worlds to conquer and strip."

"Then, that should mean they're not

interested in us," Cullen said. "If they've been traveling in space as long as you say, they surely have long range scanning capability, and they must know that other than yakbeasts, saurofowls, guggle melons . . . and juju beans, there are no resources of any value here on End of the Line. We have breathable air and water, and that's about it."

Frank seemed looked at Cullen across the rim of his cup. His expression told Cullen that he was internally debating something, something important. Finally, his tense face relaxed as he seemed to come to some important decision.

"We think the G'rok want M13-, er End of the Line, for the same reason Flight Commander Pisante and the rest of the high command want it . . . its location makes it a perfect jumping off point for invading either system. They haven't shared their plans with me, but I think IDF wants to turn your planet into a base for invasion of the G'rok system. Our long range scans show that while their planets are having shortages of food, they're rich with certain important elements we need in our industry."

It didn't make Cullen happy to know he'd guessed right. What it did was depress him. To think that his species was no better than a bunch of lizards made him very, very sad.

"So," he said. "We find ourselves in the path of *two* invaders, not one. If they establish a base here, they'll have to move all the civilians off planet, won't they?"

Frank nodded sadly. "I'm afraid so," he said. "That is, all the ones that are left after the G'rok invade."

"What do you mean by that?" Bitsy's eyes were wide as she spoke.

Cullen frowned. He had an idea what Frank's answer would be, and it made him mad.

"Well," Frank said. "The commander sort of knew coming in that the G'rok would get here ahead of our guys. We don't know the specifics of what they do because they cut off all communications, but it's pretty likely that most of the population will be killed. He was hoping that the G'rok would be distracted after taking over, and we'd be able to swoop in and defeat them while they were on the planet."

Cullen made a growling sound deep in his throat. "So, Pisante knew we'd be wiped out. Why'd he even bother coming in to talk to us? He could have just waited until the G'rok did their business, and then come in."

Frank looked down at the floor. When he lifted his head and looked from Bitsy to Cullen, he had tears in his eyes.

"It's because of a clause in the Federation Code," he said. "In order to establish a base on an independent planet, we need the agreement of the planetary government unless it's already an official member of the

Federation. You guys never joined. And, even if one person survived the G'rok attack, if we didn't have an agreement, it wouldn't matter that we came in and defeated the G'rok after the invasion. We'd need to get the agreement, or after defeating them, we'd have to pull back. Under the circumstances, it's hardly likely the survivors would be to amenable to granting basing rights, so Commander Pisante figured to come in ahead of the G'rok, get the agreement, and then leave, . . . coming back after they arrived and done whatever it is they do."

Bitsy's face paled. Cullen's angry scowl deepened.

"Why, that dirty son of a . . . I ought to go out to your ship and ram a fist down his throat," Cullen said.

"Look, for what it's worth, not everyone in the IDF agrees with this plan," Frank said. "I think it's a pretty underhanded way to treat people, and I'm sorry."

"No need for you to apologize." Cullen stood. He walked around the desk and laid a hand on Frank's shoulder. "You took a big risk telling us this, and I appreciate it. You probably ought to get back to your ship before Pisante gets suspicious."

"What do you plan to do?"

Cullen looked at Bitsy and smiled. "First things first," he said. "We got to prepare for the arrival of the G'rok."

Charles Ray

TEN

After Frank left, Bitsy looked across at Cullen. "Okay, Mr. Smarty Pants," she said. "Just how are we supposed to defend our planet against aliens who have already taken several planets?"

"I'm still working that out," he said. "It sort of depends on what they do. If they come in guns ablazing from space, there's probably not much we can do . . . other than hide in the caves, I guess. I'm kinda hoping maybe they'll talk first before shooting."

"What makes you think they'll want to talk?"

What indeed? He hadn't a clue as to what kind of creatures these G'roks were, other than they were descended from lizards like the great monsters that ruled the planet Earth before being made extinct by a meteor striking the planet and destroying their environment. The saurofowl on End of the Line were small versions of the giant lizards of Earth, and they were, in addition to having tasty meat, family oriented creatures. A pair of saurofowl mated for life, and never abandoned their young, which was why it was so easy to hunt them in the wild. Even the domesticated version tended to pair off and jealously guarded their nests. So, if the G'rok shared the traits of the lizard-like creatures with which he was familiar, they would be reasonable. Not the emotionless killers that people assumed cold-blooded creatures to be. He mentally crossed his fingers in the hope that he was right.

"Just a feeling," he said in answer to Bitsy's question. "But, to be on the safe side, we need to get everyone into the caves."

"That's not going to be easy," she said.

That, Cullen discovered after he'd convinced Moira to call the council back into session, was an understatement.

"You were supposed to decide whether or not the fops could set up a base here," Chang said. "Why should we have to close our businesses and go underground?"

"Yeah," Jackson chimed in. "I'm in the middle of harvest season right now. If I stop, I'll lose a good bit of my crop."

Cullen had insisted that Bitsy be included in the meeting, the first time she'd been included in the colony's deliberations. As she looked around the table, she was not impressed with what she saw and heard.

"Would you rather lose your lives?" she asked innocently.

That brought an abrupt halt to everyone's outbursts Mouths hung open as they stared at her.

"Look, I know this isn't an easy thing to do," Cullen said. "But, we need to make sure everyone's protected when these G'rok arrive."

"But, it's the IDF's job to protect us," Gonzales said.

Hajib dipped her head in agreement. Moira sat at her usual position and looked from one to another face, smiling faintly when her gaze fell upon Cullen. The smile her fleshy lips made, though, wasn't matched by the look in her eyes. She looked scared.

"In this case," Cullen said. "The IDF is in no position to help. The G'rok will have done their business long before the IDF ships arrive."

"B-but, that Pisante fellow said-"

"He lied," Cullen cut her off. "He just wanted to get an agreement to put a base here, so they could use it to invade the G'rok Empire. He doesn't care what happens to us."

She looked plaintively at Cullen. "S-so, what do we do?"

"We get everyone to safety, and I'll try to figure out what to do about the G'rok."

"Where is it safe?" Little Elk asked.

"Well, there's an ice storage cave behind this place that should hold everyone in town," he said. He turned to look at Jackson and Gonzales. "And, I know you both have caves on your places. All the outlying residents should fit in them."

"Where will you be?" Moira asked.

"I'll be at my repair yard. I got a small cave there if things get dicey."

"We'll be there," Bitsy said.

There'd been a bit more argument, but it was desultory. No one who knew Cullen could ever accuse him of being the emotional type, or a person given to scare-mongering. If he thought they should hide, they would hide. Moira Nakitomi seemed relieved that he was willing to assume full responsibility. He was a bit put out that Bitsy had insisted on remaining with him, but not surprised.

Pisante and Frank were waiting for them when they arrived back at the repair yard.

"Has your council made a decision on establishing a base here?" Pisante asked.

"They've left it to me to decide," Cullen said. "And, I think I'd like to wait and see what happens with these aliens."

"That's a foolhardy course of action." Pisante's voice was as hard as flint. "You're putting everyone on the planet at risk."

"Seems to me, we're at risk no matter

what decision I make." Cullen's tone was equally hard. "Unless you're saying you won't defend us unless I agree to your proposal?"

"N-no, I'm not saying that."

"He couldn't say that," Frank said. "IDF rules are pretty clear. We have to come to the defense of any planet within Federation space, whether or not it's formally a member of the Federation."

Pisante frowned at his deputy. Frank kept a blank look on his face, but his cheeks darkened when Bitsy smiled and winked at him.

"Ahem, well yes, Lieutenant Frank's correct," Pisante said. "We'll do what we can to defend the planet, but I'm afraid the G'rok will arrive before IDF forces do, so there's nothing we can do to help before then. In fact, I believe it's time we were taking off."

"If it's okay with you, sir," Frank said. "I think I'd like to stay here and help Mr. Park with the planet's defense."

Pisante eyed his deputy suspiciously, looking from him to Bitsy. It was clear to Cullen that as foolish as the man might be about a lot of things, he wasn't fooled by Frank's excuse for wanting to stay on the planet. After a few seconds, he shrugged.

"Very well, Mr. Frank," he said. "You are hereby assigned to ground defense duties. Good luck."

He spun on his heels and started back toward their ship. When he was about halfway there, one of the crew members, who had remained the whole time in the ship, stuck his head through the exit.

"Commander Pisante," the man said in a frantic voice. "Our scanners just picked up several large ships about to enter orbit around the planet."

"Our ships arrived early, have they?" Pisante said hopefully.

"N-no, sir," the man said. "They're coming from the wrong direction to be ours. S-sir, I think it's the G'rok."

Pisante stopped midstride. His head swiveled around. He had a look of panic on his face. He then started walking again, at a faster pace, toward the ship. "P-prepare for immediate take off," he said.

"Sir, if we take off now, they'll be sure to spot us, and I don't think we can outrun them."

Pisante stopped again. He turned, his hands at his sides, a confused look on his face.

"W-what will we do?" he asked no one in particular. "W-we're t-trapped here."

Cullen strode forward until he was beside the now quivering IDF officer. Frank and Bitsy followed close behind.

"Appears to me," Cullen said. "That we oughta be getting that ship of yours under cover so they don't spot it."

Pisante's lips were moving, but no sound came forth, only a small thread of spittle from the corner of his mouth. His face was the color of old parchment too long exposed to light, and his eyes were unfocused.

"Not a bad idea," Frank said. "But, how do we hide even a vessel this size."

"Well, this is a parts yard," Bitsy said. "A junkyard, actually. If we piled a lot of junk around it, they might mistake it for just one more piece of junk."

Cullen resented his place being called a junkyard, but he had to admit that Bitsy's idea made sense.

"Okay. Morley, could you get the crew to help us move stuff?"

Frank nodded and jogged over to the ship. He spoke to the crewman in the door, and shortly four IDF troopers dressed in the uniforms of flight crew came out and followed him to where Cullen stood. Cullen assigned Bitsy to direct them. He put a hand on Pisante's arm.

"Come on, commander," he said gently. "I think we'd better get you inside. You look too much like what you are, and I don't think we can disguise you, so we'll have to put you under wraps."

Pisante didn't protest or resist as Cullen led him into the office. He helped him up onto one of the barrels, patted his shoulder and went back outside.

In a very short time, a significant pile of spare parts, some coated with months of rust and grime, had grown around the IDF ship. It wouldn't fool anyone looking closely on the ground, but from space it would be hard to tell that a working space ship was nestled in the pile of . . . Cullen had to admit it, junk.

He patted Frank on the shoulder and smiled at Bitsy. "Good job, guys," he said.

"The G'rok will be entering orbit in a few minutes," Frank said. "The crew will stay in the ship, monitoring things." He held up a wrist communicator. "They'll keep me advised of what they're seeing. I think we maybe ought to go inside."

Back inside the office, they saw that Pisante hadn't moved from where Cullen had left him. He sat there hugging himself and rocking back and forth, a vacant look on his face.

"Looks like he's totally out of it," Cullen said.

"I was afraid this would happen," Frank said. "This is his first space assignment. He's been a desk jockey his entire career, but he needed an assignment out here in order to be qualified for promotion to admiral. First sign of trouble, though, and he freaks."

"Well, at least he can't cause any trouble," Bitsy said. "So, now what do we do about the trouble we have up there." She pointed upwards.

Frank's wrist communicator buzzed.

He held it to his ear. The tinny voice was barely audible to Cullen.

"Lieutenant, we're reading five large vessels in orbit above the planet . . . wait . . . there's a smaller vessel breaking away from them, and it just entered the planet's atmosphere. It's heading this way."

"Does it look like it's hostile?" Frank asked.

"No, Sir. Looks like a scout ship."

"Okay, keep monitoring. Advise us if the ships in orbit make any hostile moves." Frank turned to Cullen. "How do you want to handle this?"

Cullen had been thinking on that issue. The fact that the G'rok hadn't just bombarded them from space told him they had a chance. And, he remembered something he'd heard in school many cycles past—a trait of cold-blooded animals—that might help them to end the invasion of End of the Line before it started.

"Let's go out and welcome our visitors," he said.

Charles Ray

ELEVEN

Just outside the office, Cullen stopped and turned to Bitsy. "You remember that hose and pump contraption I was working on down by the cave?" he asked.

"Sure," she replied. "You were planning to air condition the office."

"Well, I want you to run down and hook it up. Then turn the pump on full blast."

She looked confused at first. Then, her lips turned up in a wicked smile. She hurried away.

"What was that all about?" Frank asked.

"I'll explain it later," Cullen said. He looked up. A bright object was rapidly descending toward the lot, riding on a column of blue flame. "Our friends are about to arrive. Let's you and me go greet them."

Inside the descending scout ship, K'rket

looked intently at the view screen which showed the haphazard arrangement of the terrain below them. Piles of objects, some of which he recognized as space ship parts, were scattered about randomly. As they neared the surface, he saw three figures emerge from a small boxlike structure. One, smaller than the other two, went off toward a mound of dirt and rock, while the other two continued in the direction of the spot the pilot had selected for landing.

His two escorts, who also served as pilot and navigator of the craft, were silent as befitted individuals of their status. If he wanted to hear from them, he would let them know. He didn't particularly care, though, to hear from them. His thoughts were on what he would do when the craft landed, and he met the warm blooded denizens of this planet.

The previous planets they'd invaded had been relatively easy pickings. Only one had put up any resistance—a group of not-yet-adult warm bloods had thrown rocks at his ship after it landed. A few well-placed laser beams bracketing them and melting the ground around them had shown them the error of their ways. Their elders had quite quickly capitulated. In all the others, most of the population near the landing site had come out to demonstrate that they had no hostile intent, and takeover had proceeded without a shot being fired.

Intelligence had indicated that the current target was sparsely populated. Nonetheless, it seemed a bit strange to only see two individuals meeting his ship. He'd expected more. Oh well, he thought, these descendants of monkeys were hard to fathom, as capricious as their simian ancestors. He would deal with them.

He noticed a flat and mostly unobstructed area near a large pile of debris. He stabbed that point on the navigation screen with a scaly finger. At the pilot's console, a small screen beeped and lit up, providing him with landing coordinates. The pilot ducked his shoulders and dipped his head in acknowledgement. He stabbed a few buttons on the panel. Lights in the cabin flickered and turned red. A harsh buzzing sound announced the impending contact with the planet's surface. K'rket braced himself for landing.

Cullen and Frank watched the craft slow its descent. The blue tail upon which it rode flickered. Closer now, they could see that it was a bulbous aircraft, not suited for quick maneuvering. There were no signs of weaponry on the bilious green surface, which looked like the scales of an overweight snake.

As it neared the surface, a roar assaulted their ears. At about five hundred meters above the surface, the roar changed to a high, piercing whine, and the blue flame from the engine nozzles changed to orange. Spindly landing legs snaked from the sides of the aircraft, which was about the same size as Pisante's craft.

The G'rok hadn't opened fire, which indicated they might want to talk first. No, Cullen reassured himself, they *must* want to talk first. Else, why would they send an apparently unarmed craft to the surface so openly? Even knowing this, though, he couldn't help but remember what his grandfather told him about how he felt the first time the hijacked prison ship he piloted approached the planet.

"You sure we have enough fuel to make the planet, Tony?" Joseph Little Elk asked. "Maybe we ought to aim for the largest moon."

The two men peered at the viewport, which showed the planet that the astrolibrary had identified as M1319X along with its two moons.

"No," Tongsu 'Tony' Park said. "We're going for the planet. We know it's habitable, but despite the appearance of water, the astrolibrary is silent on the habitability of the moons."

"We only get one shot," Little Elk said.

"Don't worry about it. We'll make it, trust me." Park wished, though, that he felt as confident as he sounded.

Ever since overpowering the guards and

crew, with the help of Little Elk, Hector Gonzales, Laura Jacobs, and Henry Jackson, and putting them in an escape pod programmed to return to the Lunar Colony launch pad, they'd been heading farther into the unexplored regions at the edge of the galaxy. Except for the nearly cryptic entries in the astrolibrary, they knew little of the area toward the prison ship flew—only that it had to be better than the prison station in the asteroid belt to which they'd originally been consigned.

Of the thirty-two prisoners on the ship, only six had been convicted of violent crimes, but all had received what amounted to life sentences. Scuttlebutt had it that prisoners sent to the asteroid belt to mine precious minerals from the orbiting rocks were on a one-way journey. No one knew anyone who had ever returned. Asteroid mining was dirty and dangerous work, Park had heard. The life expectancy of an asteroid miner was about six months. A slip with a laser drill, a corrupted air hose, either of which could be aided by a fellow prisoner with a grudge, and it was over.

He'd decided before the ship left lunar orbit that he would die trying to escape rather than be stuck in the perpetual darkness of an asteroid mine, breathing recycled air and consuming his own recycled waste.

The five of them had been prisoners

together for the nine months they'd been in the Lunar Station jail, and had developed the closest thing to friendship possible for someone on the wrong side of the law. During the first few weeks of the outward voyage, they'd talked casually at first of escape, but as the days wore on, the talk became more serious. Their chance had come when the guards, assuming that petty conmen and thieves weren't dangerous, had let their vigilance lapse. There'd only been two guards, and they were overpowered in minutes. When the crew of three realized that the prisoners now controlled everything but the cockpit, and taking Park's word that if they surrendered they wouldn't be harmed, had given up the ship. The five officials had been given knock-out drops and put in cryobeds in one of the ship's escape pods, and Park, the only one among the prisoners who had ever piloted a vessel, had taken the helm.

Now, two weeks into their escape, M1369X grew larger on the screens. They would soon be within its gravitational pull, and he would have to find a suitable landing spot and commit to bringing the ship down. It would be a one-way trip, although only Little Elk knew that. There was just enough fuel left in the tanks to get them down to the surface, and then it would be bone dry. They'd decided to keep this from the others to avoid panic, or worse.

"I guess I should go back and get the

others prepared for landing," Little Elk said.

"Yeah, Joe, you do that. I'll try to bring it down as softly as possible."

"You ever land one a ship this size before?"

"Uh, well . . . I landed a one-man survey ship . . . once."

Little Elk laughed. "Oh hell, beggars can't be choosers, I guess. That's better than what any of the rest of us have ever done. Okay, pardner, see you dirt side."

Still laughing, Little Elk left the cockpit, leaving Park alone with his thoughts. And, dark thoughts they were. He *had* landed a survey ship once. It was the year he turned sixteen. He'd stolen the thing from the yard where his father worked and taken it for a joyride around Luna Colony, before crashing it into one of the craters while trying to evade the colony's police flitters. He'd walked away from the wreckage with a busted collarbone and bruises over most of his body, and for his sins had spent six weeks in juvenile detention, assigned to clean out the toilet expulsion chutes. An ignominious start to his criminal career, and a story he'd not shared with Little Elk, who was as close to a best friend to him as anyone had ever been. With luck, he would never have to share it.

And, luck was something he was going to need a lot of if they were to survive. His first task would be to locate a suitable landing spot on the planet, and then, he'd have to get the ship down—hopefully in one piece.

It had all seemed so easy when they were bundling the guards and crew in the escape pod. Now, though, with the planet becoming larger in the view screen, doubts began to creep in. He felt cold all over, and he couldn't shake the images in his mind of the craft pancaking into the planet, exploding, and converting all on board into their component atoms.

Oh well, he thought, life's a one-way trip anyway, and it always ends at the same destination. He began the pre-orbital procedure. That went smoothly, but as he took it lower, the ship began to buck and shimmy as it entered the upper stratosphere of the planet. He knew that as it went lower into the thicker atmosphere, it would only get worse.

"Well, one way or another," he said to himself. "This is the end of the line."

The G'rok ship was low enough now to kick up dust. Cullen and Frank protected their eyes with their hands as it settled to the surface. After a few seconds, it stopped swaying and the engine sound dropped to a soft whine, and then silence.

They watched, but for a long time, other than the clicking sound of the ship's metal plates contracting as they cooled, nothing happened.

After what seemed like hours, but in

reality was less than two minutes, a hatch in the side of the ship opened and a set of landing steps extended downward. From the dark interior a figure not much larger than Cullen appeared. The figure wore a heavy suit that looked like it was made of thin rubber tires stacked one atop the other, and over that was a large round helmet with dark goggles where eyes would be. The figure walked smoothly down the steps and toward Cullen and Frank.

The figure stopped about six meters from them. It checked a gauge on its left wrist, and then reached up and removed the helmet.

Frank gasped. Cullen stared, but was silent. He imagined that he and Frank looked as strange to the creature as it did to them. It had a blunt snout with nostril holes above a thin-lipped mouth. Above that were two narrow eyes, black ovals against yellow. The lids didn't blink as it regarded them for several seconds, but once, an opaque nictating membrane slide in from the outer edges of each eye.

The creature reached up to the collar and pressed a large black button on its left shoulder. There was a hissing sound and a few clicks, and then a nasal voice came from a dark circle just below the creature's throat.

"Greetings, warm-blooded ones," the voice said. "I am Supreme Broodmaster K'rket of the G'rok Empire. I am here to discuss the terms of your surrender."

Charles Ray

TWELVE

"Welcome, Supreme Broodmaster K'rket of the G'rok Empire. I am Military Liaison Cullen Park of the Planet End of the Line, and this is Lieutenant Morley Frank of the Interstellar Defense Force of the Federation of Planets," Cullen said, bowing low. "We can go into my office to discuss the terms of our relationship."

K'rket grimaced, causing Cullen and Frank to shrink back, until the lizard-like being spoke, "Very well put, human—that is your species, is it not?—we Saurians appreciate dealing with those who know proper etiquette."

So, Cullen thought, that must have been a smile. Crikey, I'd hate to see what he looks like when he's angry. Cullen smiled, careful to keep his mouth closed so his teeth didn't show, and stepped aside, waving toward his office.

"This way, if you please," he said. "Will your crew be joining us?"

"No," K'rket said. "They will wait in the ship until we have concluded our business."

They entered to find Pisante sitting in the same position that Cullen had left him in. When he saw the Saurian enter, his eyes went wide and his face paled. "Wha-"

"This is Supreme Broodmaster Cricket," Cullen said. "He's a Saurian from a planet called G'rok—he's also called a G'rok—it's all a bit confusing, but he's here to talk some kind of deal."

K'rket looked from Cullen to Pisante. The opaque membranes in his eyes slid back and forth.

"Who is this creature?" he asked.

"This," Cullen said. "Is Flight Commander Gregory Pisante, and he is Lieutenant Frank's commanding officer."

K'rket inclined his head slightly, his eyes boring through Pisante, who stared back with a goggle-eyed expression of disbelief. K'rket turned back to Cullen.

"I will forgive you the mispronunciation of my name," he said. "It is K'rket. You warm bloods do not seem to have the proper vocalization mechanisms to make the correct sound. I am to assume that you are the one in charge here." It wasn't a question.

"That's correct," Cullen said. "Sorry for mangling your moniker. Kri . . . K'rket. There, did I get it right?"

"Yes, but it is never to be spoken without the full title."

"Ah, yes, right . . . Supreme Broodmaster K'rket. Would you like a drink before we start our palaver?"

The translation device at his throat chirped and whirred. K'rket's scaly head swung from side to side. Then, his eyes widened, showing a large amount of yellow which Cullen found quite unsettling.

"I understand," K'rket said. "You wish to offer a libation before we commence our talks. Kamsahamnida, I will accept a libation."

Cullen smiled. He wondered who had programmed the alien's translator. The mixing of two of the Federation's lingua franca, and the use of such an archaic term as 'libation,' indicated that someone from the Federation had previously worked with the G'rok—a piece of information he filed away for later use. He took out four tin cups and filled them with juju juice. He passed one to K'rket as the guest of honor, then handed one to Pisante and Frank.

K'rket stared at the cup until Cullen took a drink. He then lifted the cup to his mouth and, tilting his head back, drained it. The nictating membranes closed over his eyes, his mouth gaped open, and his entire body quivered. Cullen stopped breathing. This wasn't good—killing the representative of the G'rok before he'd even had an opportunity to speak. Then, K'rket's mouth closed and the membranes slid aside. The grimace that represented a smile spread over his greenish face.

"My, my," he said. The translator spoke in a gravelly voice. "That is quite good. May I have another?"

"You like this stuff?" Frank asked. He looked at K'rket with a mixture of amazement and respect.

"Yes, this is very good. It is similar to a drink we have on G'rok, we call it n'galu. It is made from a plant called the n'ginku, which is quite toxic unless properly prepared. What do you call this wonderful libation, and how is it made?"

"It's called juju juice," Cullen said. "We make it from the juju bean. They're not toxic, but if it's not brewed properly, it can cause you to go blind."

"Is this libation popular throughout warm blood space?"

"No, it's not," Frank said. "Far as I know, M13-, er, End of the Line is the only place that has it. I've been all over the system, and it's the strongest drink there is."

K'rket took the second cup of juju juice and downed it as fast as he'd done the first. He immediately held his cup out for a refill. Cullen smiled as he poured. The alien couldn't be all bad, he thought. Unlike many of the spacers who visited End of the Line, he appreciated the local brew.

By the time he'd finished his fourth drink, and Cullen had opened a second bottle, the Saurian was swaying on the barrel.

"Thish ish one of the besht libations I have ever had," he said. K'rket's capacity was amazing, but it was getting to him when even his translator's speech became slurred.

Cullen also noticed that the air temperature was dropping slowly. He could feel a chill on his exposed skin. Good, he thought, Bitsy got the hose hooked up and the pump started. He hoped that the alien's thick skin wouldn't notice the gradual change in temperature.

When K'rket asked for a fifth drink— actually, held his cup out and mumbled some unintelligible sounds that his translator could only reproduce as squeaks—Cullen knew that his plan was working.

He remembered his grandfather telling him a story when he was small. A frog in a pot of water over a low flame won't notice the gradual increase in temperature, and will remain in the pot until it cooks. He remembered from his science classes that cold blooded creatures didn't actually have cold blood. Instead, their body temperature changes as the air temperature around them changes. In order to move smoothly and quickly their muscles must be warm, and they get warm, not by regulating their body temperature like mammals, but by moving to a warmer place. The cooling temperature caused K'rket's muscles to become weak and his movements to slow down, and the juju juice had affected his reasoning skills so he was incapable of moving to get warm.

Cullen watched as the alien slowly slid down from the barrel and landed in a heap on the floor. He began snoring loudly, which the translator reproduced as a sound akin to a metal saw.

Pisante and Frank looked down at the sleeping alien.

"Is he gonna be okay?" Frank asked.

"Yeah, if we warm him up pretty soon, there shouldn't be any permanent damage," Cullen said. He walked to the door and looked outside. Bitsy stood at the corner of the building. "Bitsy, can you hook up another hose and sneak it to the G'rok ship?"

"Sure, it'll take me five or ten minutes. You want me to pump cold air in slow?"

"No, hit 'em hard and fast," he said. "We need these guys knocked out fast."

"Okay, five minutes, then," she said, and turned and disappeared behind the building.

Cullen ducked back inside. "Okay, guys, as soon as Bitsy has the crew in the G'rok ship under control, the next phase of our plan goes into effect."

"Are you going to share that plan with us?" Frank asked.

Before Cullen could answer, Bitsy came in to the office. She had a wolfish smile on her face. "Didn't take five minutes," she said.

"Those guys are a lot smaller than his nibs here. One blast and they crumpled like tissue."

"Okay, folks, let's go start phase two," Cullen said. "I'll explain as we go along."

Charles Ray

THIRTEEN

Bitsy hadn't been subtle about pumping cold air into the G'rok ship. She'd merely put the hose in the door and turned the pump on full. When Cullen led everyone up the ramp and into the ship, all of the interior surfaces were covered in white rime—including the two G'rok slumped over the control panel.

Cullen eased them aside and studied the panel, looking for a communication device. Bitsy, a self-taught space engineer found what he was looking for, a large black button below a round screen off to the right. She pointed at it.

"How do I make it work?" Cullen asked.

"If I had to guess, I'd say, push to talk," Bitsy replied.

Of course, Cullen thought. The simplest way is always the best, and if the G'rok were sophisticated enough to be galactic invaders, they were sophisticated enough to know that their systems should be as simple to operate as possible. In particular, communications systems work best when they are simple and can be quickly activated.

"Okay, that makes sense," he said. "While I'm pushing this thing, why don't you get something to restrain our friends here so we can get the temperature up in here? I wouldn't want to do them any permanent damage." He reached over and pressed the black button.

There was a squawking sound, and a lot of hissing in the background. The large navigation screen, which had been transparent, turned black and then a picture appeared. At first, it seemed like a photo of a cockpit only slightly larger than the one in which they were standing, but then, a smaller, lighter green version of K'rket stepped into view. The figure's mouth moved. A hissing sound came out of the walls. The figure touched a button below its throat, and the hissing became high pitched speech, "I am First Officer L'tel, and-" The figure calling itself L'tel looked at Cullen with its eyes wide. "Where are the members of the crew, and where is Supreme Broodmaster K'rket? And, who or what are you?"

"That's a lot of questions there, First Officer Little," Cullen said. He stepped aside to let L'tel see Bitsy wrapping the ship's crew with black, sticky duct tape, a commodity that she always had two or three rolls of on her person. "We're making sure your crew is comfortable, but not able to get into any trouble. As for . . . Supreme Broodmaster Cricket, he's my guest in my office until we can come to an understanding."

The poor creature looked confused. His mouth opened and closed as if he was gasping for air. "I do not comprehend," he said. "Why are you restraining the crew? I need to speak with Supreme Broodmaster *K'rket*."

"Okay, I'll talk to him and get back to you." Cullen pressed the black button again, and was rewarded by the screen going black. Just before it did, though, he was further rewarded by the look he interpreted to be shock on L'tel's face. When he turned, he was elated to see a look of confusion of Pisante's face.

"Mr. Park," Pisante said. "Do you mind enlightening us as to what the bloody hell you're doing?"

"What I'm trying to do, Mr. Pissant, is stop an invasion." Cullen knew his mispronunciation of the man's name infuriated him, but he frankly didn't give a fig at that point. Now that he knew that Pisante was willing to sacrifice the lives of everyone on End of the Line—for reasons Cullen still didn't understand—he saw no reason for even pretending to be cooperative.

"Stopping the invasion is the job of the

IDF," Pisante said.

"Yeah, but I've figured out that what you want to do is stop the G'rok from invading the rest of the system *from* End of the Line," Cullen said. "I plan on stopping 'em from taking over here in the first place."

"Hah, you think one man can stop an entire fleet of invading aliens? I'd love to know how you plan to do that. And, I've told you before; my name is PEE-SAHNT, not piss ant."

Cullen snorted. "Right, sorry, I forgot." He turned to Frank and smiled. "Let's go back to my office, well, I guess now it's planetary defense headquarters, and plan our next step."

"I don't know what you're up to, but it sounds like it'll be fun," Frank said. He smiled broadly.

"Lieutenant Frank," Pisante said. "I think you should think twice before you associate yourself too closely with this man. I think he's heading for failure, and I don't think it will be good for your career."

Frank stopped. He turned and faced his commander, his hands on his hips. "With all due respects, sir, we're kind of stuck here right now, with no place to go. If Cullen's plan fails, my career won't really matter, because we'll all probably be dead."

Cullen clapped him on the shoulder. "Hey, Morley, you gotta have more faith than that."

"I have faith in you, my friend, but I just don't think we have enough to fight off those G'rok ships up there in space."

"Who said anything about fighting," Cullen said. "My grandpa always said the best way to win a fight is not to fight it in the first place. If I've read these lizards right, we might be able to stop their invasion right here without a shot being fired."

"You are a foolish young man," Pisante said.

"But, I'm willing to listen to how you plan to do it," Frank said.

"Good, let's go into my . . . headquarters, and have some more juju juice while I describe it to you." He turned toward the G'rok ship, where Bitsy was just coming down the landing ramp. "Bitsy, when you get that thing warmed up again and you've checked to make sure those fellas are okay, join us in my office."

Charles Ray

FOURTEEN

Cullen, Bitsy, and Frank sat on barrels around the crate Cullen used as a desk, two opened bottles of juju juice in the center of the crate. Pisante sat on the fourth barrel in the corner next to the still unconscious K'rket, hugging himself tightly against the chill that still hung in the air in the room.

Bitsy took a long drink from her cup. Frank watched her with his eyes agog. "How does a tiny thing like you drink that stuff?" he asked.

"Here on End of the Line we start drinking this stuff as soon as we're off mother's milk. It's an acquired taste."

Frank took a sip, coughing as he forced it down his throat. "I'm not sure I'll ever really *acquire* it, I'm afraid. I sure wish I had some beer."

"Sorry, buddy," Cullen said. "We don't grow the grains here you need to brew anything resembling beer. It's not all that bad, is it?"

Frank stared at his cup. "I'll bet this stuff could power a space ship." He tossed back the contents of his cup. "But, I guess it'll have to do. Now, how are you going to get the G'rok not to fight?"

Cullen refilled Frank's cup, drained his, and refilled it. After taking a drink, he wiped his mouth with his sleeve. "Well, it's like this," he said. "I kinda figure these lizards don't do anything without orders. This guy, Cricket, is the big cheese with this bunch, so if I keep him under wraps, they'll just sit up there waiting."

"Then what?"

"Well, I haven't figured out that part yet. But, I'm working on it."

Frank leaned toward Bitsy. "Is he always like this . . . making up things as he goes along?"

Bitsy drained her cup and poured another. "Pretty much," she said. "I know it seems a little loose. I guess you IDF guys are used to having everything all planned out in advance. In that, you're not too different from the lizards." Frank's cheeks colored. "Oh, you're different, though, Morley. You seem capable of thinking outside the lines. That's the way Cullen operates, and it always seems to work."

"Hm, if you trust him, I guess I do too. So, we just wait until the next inspiration hits him?"

"I have an idea," Cullen said. "I think I know what we have to do next, but we have to wake old Cricket up to do it."

Charles Ray

FIFTEEN

Pisante shot off the barrel. "I object to you doing that," he said. "I don't think your plan has a chance of working, but at least with the leader incommunicado, the G'rok fleet will sit there until the IDF arrives, and we can annihilate them."

Cullen looked over at Pisante. "Oh, I plan to have this whole shebang settled long before your IDF studs get here, flight commander, so you just sit back down and calm yourself."

"You, you can't do this."

Cullen stood up, walked around the desk and leaned over until his face was almost touching Pisante's.

"Actually, little man," he said. "I can do it.

The council put me in charge of this situation. I remind you that you're a visitor on our planet, and you got no say in what we do."

"B-but, I'm a senior officer in IDF. I'm responsible for planetary defense." Pisante backed away, but Cullen followed, keeping his nose a few millimeters from Pisante's.

"You're responsible for a planet's defense under the authority of the planetary government," Cullen said. "I remember a little from the classes in civics we were required to take in school. When a planet is not a formal member of the Federation, you're under the *command* of the planetary authorities." He turned to Bitsy. "Did I get that right, Bitsy?"

"You sure did, Cullen. I thought you were sleeping through most of your classes. Guess I was wrong."

Cullen smiled and winked at her. "Now, Mr. IDF officer, it's like this. According to End of the Line's Council, I'm the planetary official responsible for military liaison. They didn't exactly specify what that meant—in fact, they sorta left it to me to define it—so I think it means I'm responsible for anything having to do with the military. And, since they didn't say only IDF, I'm responsible for dealing with the G'rok military as well."

"B-b-but-"

"I think he has you there, sir," Frank said to the stammering Pisante. "Unless *you* plan on invading and taking over the planet, seems like Cullen . . . Mr. Park is in charge and we have to follow his orders."

Pisante seemed to shrink in upon himself. He stopped backing up when his narrow butt hit the barrel upon which he'd been sitting. Cullen, seeing the expression on the little man's face, felt sorry for him. He backed away.

"So, you see," he said. "We're doing it my way. Bitsy, go turn the pump off so this place warms up and our friend, Mr. Cricket wakes up."

Pisante levered himself upon the barrel and sat there with his arms folded across his scrawny chest.

"Well, Lieutenant Frank, if you wish to follow this unwashed provincial, I don't suppose I can stop you, but I will have nothing to do with what I believe to be a scatterbrained plan."

"B-but, flight commander," Frank said. "How can you call Cullen's plan scatterbrain? You haven't even heard it yet. I mean, he did manage to capture the G'rok commander and disable their ship without firing a shot. I think he deserves to at least be heard."

Pisante made a sniffing sound and turned his head away. Frank looked at him imploringly, but to no avail. The little officer was adamant. Turning, Frank looked at Cullen and shrugged.

"Not to worry," Cullen said. "Bitsy, go ahead and turn the pump off. Let's get some heat in here."

Bitsy mock-saluted Cullen and, with a wink at Frank, scampered off.

Very quickly the temperature in the small room began to rise. As the temperature inched upwards, K'rket began to twitch and then squirm. Bubbling sounds came from between his lips. Cullen bent over to watch, but kept well back. He didn't know what G'rok personal defensive mechanisms were, and couldn't be sure how the creature would react upon awakening, so he took no chances.

At last, the opaque membranes over K'rket's eyes retracted. The yellow of his pupils was laced with fine red lines.

"How are you feeling, Supreme Broodmaster K'rket?" Cullen asked softly.

K'rket winced and drew back against the wall. "It is not required that you speak in such a loud voice, please," he said. "My cranial cavity suffers from some manner of abuse."

It took Cullen a second to realize that K'rket was suffering from an ailment that he was all too familiar with after a night of drinking juju juice. He had a hangover, and from the plaintive sound of his voice and the network of broken capillaries in his eyes it was one lollapalooza of a hangover.

"Sorry," he said. "I guess you had a little too much juju juice. It's something you have to gradually adapt to."

The nictating membranes closed, opened, closed, and opened again. "My condition is due to the libation you provided me?"

"I'm afraid so. You have a hangover."

"What is this . . . hangover?"

"It's what happens after you drink too much juju juice," Cullen said. "It's only temporary, but until it goes away, you'll have headaches and you'll feel like yakbeast dung. I imagine it feels like saurofowl have made a nest in your mouth too?"

"If by that you mean it feels as if I have ingested b'ulbell plants, thorns and all, yes that is precisely the sensation I am experiencing at the moment. My hearing organs also appear to be hypersensitive."

Cullen squatted and put his hands on his knees.

"Yeah, I know how you're feeling. Been that way many a morning myself."

"Is there a palliative for this condition?"

"Well, Bitsy here disagrees with me," Cullen said. "But, the thing I've found that eases the pain is just to stay drunk. Back on old Earth they called it having a bit of the hair of the dog that bit you. It'll go away by itself after a few hours. The only other cure is never to get drunk in the first place."

K'rket's long, narrow pink tongue flickered out over his nearly lipless mouth, and the opaque membranes closed again. When they opened, he looked at Cullen.

"I would not be willing to forego this

libation of yours . . . this juju juice. We have nothing like it on my world. So, it would appear that my only recourse is to do as you say, and have some of the fur of the canine that attacked me."

"You want another drink of juju juice?"

"Did I not just say that?"

SIXTEEN

K'rket pulled himself into an upright position, and, limping like an old man, made his way to Cullen's desk. He braced himself on the edge of the crate while Cullen poured another cup of juju juice, which he snatched away as soon as it was full and threw down his throat, spilling only a few drops. He held the cup out for a refill, and Cullen complied. The second cup was half-emptied in a gulp. K'rket took several deep breaths, and his mouth crinkled in what Cullen now recognized as a smile.

"You are correct," K'rket said. "That provides instant relief. I like this . . . hair of the dog."

"It always works for me," Cullen said.

"Now, though, there's some business we need to discuss."

K'rket paused with the cup halfway to his mouth. He stared at Cullen over the rim. Then, he smiled and put the cup down.

"Very well, warm blooded one," he said. "But, before we can conduct official negotiations we must exchange official titles. I am Supreme Broodmaster K'rket, son of K'lel and one thousandth in line for the throne of G'rok." He picked the cup up and drained its contents.

Cullen refilled his own cup. "I'm Cullen Andrew Park, son of Jubilee Park and grandson of Tongsu Park. I am selected by the Council of End of the Line as Military Liaison." He copied K'rket's action and downed the contents of his cup.

"Very well Cullen Andrew Park. We are now negotiators for our respective empires. Since that effectively makes us equal in rank, you may address me as K'rket."

"I'm just Cullen to my friends," Cullen said. "And, I'm really hoping we can be friends."

K'rket looked around the room. "Should our negotiations not be conducted in privacy, Cullen?"

"Oh, Bitsy here's my assistant, and I don't keep anything from her. This fella here's Morley Frank, and he's sort of my military advisor. I reckon it's okay for them to hear what we say."

K'rket pointed to Pisante who, despite the raised temperature, still hugged himself as if cold and who refused to make eye contact with any of them.

"What of this sickly looking creature?" he asked.

"Oh, him," Cullen said. "He's not part of our team, so I reckon he'll have to leave." This got Pisante's attention. He looked up and glared malevolently at Cullen. "You can go out and wait in that pile of junk near your ship."

Cullen tapped his wrist and stared at Pisante. The IDF officer stared back, then his brows arched as he realized that Cullen was trying to send him a message. He tapped the communicator on his own wrist, and Cullen nodded.

"Yes," he said. "I suppose it would be inappropriate for me to be present during such sensitive negotiations. I'll just go outside and play in the junk."

Leave it to the man, Cullen thought, to take a dig at him even as he deigned to be cooperative. He just hoped Pisante wouldn't do something stupid to jinx what he had planned with the G'rok.

"Okay," he said after Pisante was gone. "Let's get down to business."

Charles Ray

SEVENTEEN

·

"Very well," K'rket said. "What would you like to propose?"

The Saurian was smiling now, and even though Cullen was learning to read his facial expressions, the grimace that passed for a smile on the alien's face was still a bit unsettling.

"Before we get down to details," Cullen said. "I'd love to know just what your objectives here are."

"I will be happy to enlighten you," K'rket said. "After you have provided me with another libation."

Cullen filled both their cups. He lifted his. "Here's to successful negotiations," he said. "Pass the lips and over the gums, look out liver, here it comes."

They drank. K'rket looked at Cullen over

the rim of his cup. "What you just said . . . what does that mean?"

"It's what we call a toast. It's a wish for good luck."

"That is a quaint custom," K'rket said. "So you are wishing for good health? I like that. Of course, I do not possess these lips of which you speak, but I do have two livers, so I wish this libation a good journey in that direction."

"Uh, well . . . yeah, I guess I am wishing us good health. So, now why don't you tell me why you want to invade my planet?"

"I do not *want* to invade your planet. I have no choice." K'rket took another drink of juju juice. He was learning to sip like Cullen was doing. "The population of our system is growing faster than our current methods of food production can provide for. We need new sources of food, so the emperor has decreed that we will find new planets for that purpose."

"Hey," Cullen said. "You don't mean you plan to eat us, do you?"

K'rket recoiled and looked at Cullen with his mouth turned down. "Oh my, no," he said. "What kind of creatures do you think we are? We do not eat other sentient beings. We are vegetarians. Your planet grows certain plants that you use as foodstuffs, does it not. It grows the plants from which you manufacture this wonderful libation . . . this j'uj'u j'uice, for example. We require access to your plants."

"Wait a minute. You're just looking for places that can grow stuff you can eat?"

"That is correct. We are taking over planets and their inhabitants are then required to grow and ship foodstuffs to our system."

"You mean like slavery? I read about that in history class. It was commonly practiced on old Earth."

K'rket put his cup down and leaned forward. "What is this slavery you ask about?"

Cullen had read about it, but he wasn't sure he remembered the details correctly, and for some reason he felt that he should give this alien accurate information.

"Well, it was a long time ago that I read about it," he said. "But, I believe it was a system where some people owned other people, and made them work for them."

"I do not understand. What is owned?"

"Uh, it's like . . . Bitsy, can you help me out here? You were a much better student than I was."

Bitsy pointed to the translator device K'rket wore. "This thing is yours and yours alone, right?"

"You mean my translator? Why yes, this is reserved only for me."

"Well then, you can say that you *own* it. It belongs to you. That was what slavery was about. One person belonged to another just like your translator belongs to you."

K'rket cocked his head to one side. "I do not understand. How can a sentient being be the property of another?"

"Yeah, but didn't you say you are requiring the people on the planets you invade to grow food for you?" Cullen said. "That sounds a lot like slavery on old Earth to me. Do you leave soldiers to supervise the labor?"

"No, we do not have enough soldiers to do that, we simply tell the conquered people to grow the produce and have it available when our ships come to pick it up."

Cullen couldn't believe what he was hearing. What a way to conduct a military campaign. "And, they comply with your demands?"

"Why would they not? It is really quite generous of us, you know."

"How much food has been shipped back to your home world?"

"We have only taken over five worlds," K'rket said. "There has not been enough time for them to grow food for shipment."

Cullen had to stifle a laugh. The G'rok had a lot to learn about military conquest. "Say, how many times have you had to fire your weapons during one of these invasions?"

"We have not yet had to fire weapons," K'rket said. "Do you warm bloods fire weapons when you invade a planet?"

"Well, I've never invaded a planet, but I'm

pretty sure if we did, there'd be a lot of shooting."

K'rket took another drink. He held his cup up. Then he upended it. It was empty. "My libation seems to have been exhausted. Can you provide another?"

His body seemed to be adapting to the juju juice. He was no longer slurring his words or swaying. Cullen poured another drink.

"Okay, so you invade planets, but you don't fire a shot. You make demands, but you don't leave soldiers on the planet to make sure your demands are met. What will you do if any of the conquered planets fail to meet their quotas?"

"Why would they do such a thing? We have an agreement. They were defeated, so they must comply with the demands of the victor. Does your species not understand the rules of warfare?"

"But, those aren't the . . ." Cullen froze mid-sentence. A thought had come into his mind, a thought so radical he could hardly believe it could be true. "Have your people ever fought a war before?"

K'rket stared at Cullen. He reached for the translator at his throat and twisted it, cocking his head to one side as he did so. After a moment of puzzlement, he dipped his head.

"War, a state of open, armed, often protracted conflict carried on between nations, states, or parties. No, I suppose we have not," K'rket said. "We do, however have conflicts between individuals, but only between individuals of the same social class."

The two of them, human and alien, stared at each other for the longest time—one confused, the other confounded.

EIGHTEEN

Cullen was the first to recover. It took his brain a while to process what the Saurian had said, and he still found it hard to believe that there could be a society anywhere in the universe that had never experienced the trauma of war.

"How is it," he asked. "That your people can fight each other as individuals, but never have war between groups?"

K'rket reared back as if struck. "But that would mean that individuals of a lower class could possibly harm a member of a higher class. Why, that would be unthinkable."

"So, let me get this straight . . . your people have never even considered organized warfare?"

"Why no," K'rket said. "That would be uncivilized."

"But, you have fights between individuals . . . provided they're of the same social class?"

"Yes."

"I don't understand," Cullen said. "How can individuals fight, but the concept of individuals banding together in groups to fight never developed?"

K'rket shrugged, a difficult maneuver considering his sloped shoulders. "I suppose the fighting ritual on my world doesn't lend itself to large group participation. Would you care to see a demonstration?"

"Uh, there's no one here for you to fight. I mean, you're the only one of your kind here."

"Not an actual fight," the Saurian said. "Just a simple demonstration of how we do it."

"Well sure, go ahead . . . as long as no one gets hurt."

"Oh, no one ever actually gets hurt in our fights," K'rket said. And, then he stretched his head upwards and faced Cullen head-on. Two fan-like structures emerged from the sides of his neck, spreading outward and upward and shimmering in all the colors of the spectrum. After thirty seconds of waving, quivering, and shimmering, the structures withdrew back into his neck. "That is how we fight. A female of our class watches and judges which of the two contenders has the best display, deciding the outcome of the fight, and that is how we settle our personal differences on my world."

Cullen put his hand over his mouth to keep from laughing. It was the funniest thing he'd seen in a long time. At the same time, though, it was tragic. K'rket and his kinsmen had so far only encountered unarmed earth settlements, where people had probably surrendered in fear upon seeing their lizard-like invaders. When the G'rok ships encountered IDF ships, though, it would be a different story, and would likely end up in a massacre—a massacre he would like to prevent if possible.

Bitsy, on the other hand, was enthralled at K'rket's colorful display. She clapped her hands when he was done. "That was absolutely beautiful," she said.

K'rket bowed at the waist. "Thank you Lady Bitsy," he said. "The females of my species also think I am the most colorful fighter, and as a result I am seldom challenged."

"I hate to rain on your parades, guys," Cullen said. "But, if that's all you G'roks have, when the IDF arrives, things are likely to get quite nasty."

"I do not understand," K'rket said.

"Well, in the first place, they're not likely to be impressed by your colorful display, because they'll open fire on your ships as soon as they see them."

"But, that is not the way we conduct business. We should talk first, before our display of prowess. It is uncivilized to do otherwise."

Cullen sighed. K'rket just didn't get it. But, if he—Cullen—didn't come up with a solution before the IDF arrived, he would get it, from all barrels. Then, what K'rket said gave him an idea.

"There just might be a way to settle this without anyone having to get hurt," he said.

"How are you gonna do that?" Frank asked. "As soon as our ships see the G'rok, they'll open fire. Flight Commander Pisante will see to that."

"Bear with me," Cullen said. "Listen, K'rket, this whole expedition of yours is because you guys need food on your world, right?"

"That is right."

"Do you have anything of value on your world, like . . . oh, gold or titanium, or other metals?"

K'rket pressed his translator and cocked his head. "We do have certain metals, this yellow metal gold is one, and we have iron, titanium, silver, and many others. We use very little of them, though. They are in the . . . soil, and sometimes make it difficult for us to grow food. Why do you ask?"

"We humans just happen to like some of these useless metals of yours. We've learned to produce food very well, and have more than we really need. We could come to an agreement. You provide us shiploads of your metal, and we give you shiploads of food."

"You . . . warm bloods like metals? They cannot be eaten, and except for the amount required to build ships, they are really quite useless."

"Believe me," Cullen said. "We have many uses for them. The more of it you dig up and trade to us, the more land you have available in the future to grow food. In the meantime, you can trade for enough to feed your people. It's what we call a win-win situation."

"Would this agreement also include shipments of this wonderful juju juice?"

"As much of it as you wanted." Cullen said. "The only place in this system where it's produced and consumed is here on End of the Line."

"Then, Cullen, military liaison of End of the Line, you have an agreement."

"There's just one thing. I think you need to get in your ship and hightail it out of here before the IDF arrive. If you'll give Lieutenant Frank here the names and locations of the other planets and colonies you visited, we'll inform them of the new arrangements. I think you'll find they'll be happy to ship you all the food you require."

K'rket bowed low at the waist toward Cullen. "It will be as you wish. You are the first of your species I have had the opportunity to exchange views with, or share a libation with, and please permit me to say that it has been a pleasure."

"Well, I sorta enjoyed meeting you too, K'rket. Now, Bitsy, why don't you go untie K'rket's crew so they can be on their way. Morley, you and me need to go have a chat with your boss so there's no misunderstanding about our new arrangement with the G'roks."

Frank saluted. "Yes sir, Military Liaison Park," he said. "Let's do that." He smiled broadly. "You know, I wasn't sure at first you'd be able to pull this off, but you did. You probably just prevented our first intergalactic war. More importantly, you prevented a tragedy. Commander Pisante's not gonna be too happy at not becoming a war hero, but I think the folks back at Federation headquarters will be pleased."

NINETEEN

Cullen and Frank exited his office behind Bitsy and K'rket. As the latter two approached K'rket's ship, Pisante emerged from the pile of parts covering his ship. He approached Cullen and Frank with an angry scowl on his face.

"What's going on here? Why is that alien heading for his ship? He's our prisoner," he said.

"No he's not," Cullen said. "He's now the newest trade partner with End of the Line, and he's on his way back to his fleet to take them home to let his government know the war's over."

"Before it even really started," Frank said.

"Wha, what are you two talking about?" Pisante asked, his brow furrowing in confusion.

Between them Cullen and Frank explained what had happened. Pisante looked even more confused. He gaped in open mouthed astonishment when K'rket's ship lifted on blue columns of flame and then streaked up into the darkening sky, finally vanishing in the distance.

Bitsy walked up. Cullen noticed that she stood nearer Frank than him.

"The Supreme Broodmaster asked me to tender his gratitude to you, Cullen," she said. "During the walk to his ship, he finally understood what could have happened."

"Yeah, it wouldn't have been pretty," Cullen said.

"He was also happy because now he'll be able to stop playing soldier and focus on his scientific studies, which is where his real passion lies. He said he'll be forever grateful to you for making that possible."

"Scientific studies . . . who would've thought his interests ran in that direction?"

"And, he can now propose to a lady G'rok he's had his eyes on for some time."

"Whoa," Frank said. "You got all that in a short walk from the office to his ship?"

"Sure," she said. "He's really quite nice if you take the time to get to know him . . . and, if you ask the right questions."

"If you ever consider leaving this place," Frank said. "IDF's intelligence corps would sure be interested in you."

Cullen laughed. "I think she'd probably be a better diplomat," he said. He looked pointedly at Pisante. "She would be able to stop fights instead of looking for them."

"That's for sure." Frank turned to his commander. "Well, flight commander, I guess we're no longer needed here."

"There's still the question of an IDF base here." Pisante looked at Cullen.

"Well now, I think you know the answer to that one," Cullen said. "You're free to visit any time, of course, but I don't think we need a permanent base."

"Actually," Bitsy said. "Just before he boarded his ship, K'rket said he thinks the G'rok would like establish a consulate and trade office here, and make this the center of their relationship with the Federation."

"Wow, you were busy," Cullen said.

"You'll need the approval of the Federation for that," Pisante said.

"No we won't," Bitsy said. "As an independent planet that is not formally part of the Federation, we have the authority to make that decision for ourselves."

Pisante was not to be beaten so easily. "But, what if your council disagrees—this has to go to them for approval—and, I would like to speak to them about it before they vote."

"There won't be a vote," Cullen said. "The council gave me full authority to settle this situation, and they didn't put any limits on what I could do to settle it. I've decided that making the trade agreement and allowing the G'rok to have a trade mission and consulate here is the best way to ensure peace, and that's final. What the rest of the Federation decides to do is none of my concern. If they're smart, they'll all sign on to the trade deal. It's a winner for everyone. But, if they don't that just means a bigger slice of pie for us."

Cullen's voice was steely and his expression was like stone. Now, Pisante knew that he was well and truly defeated. He would not get basing rights on the planet. He would not be lauded as the military leader who defeated an alien invasion—that honor would go to a backwater provincial, and a civilian to boot. Most devastating of all, though, is that he would *not* be promoted to admiral. He would spend the rest of his time in IDF in desk jobs, doing meaningless work, to retire into obscurity. Life, he thought, had done its worse.

"Flight commander," Frank said. "I'm coming up on the end of my hitch. I wonder if I could stay here on End of the Line . . . I could be the military liaison between the planet and IDF until my hitch is over."

Bitsy's mouth dropped open. "You want to stay here?"

"If you want me to."

Her answer was to link arms with him and lay her head against his arm.

Pisante was totally deflated. Life hadn't done its worse. Now, he would have to explain the defection of his second in command. "Very well, lieutenant," he said. "If that's your wish. I think I'll be going now."

He walked dejectedly toward the break in the pile of parts to enter his ship. One of the crew appeared in the gap.

"Sir, our scanners indicate that the enemy fleet has moved away. They went back the way they came. Does that mean the invasion is off?"

"Yes, that's what it means," Pisante said. "Have you heard from our ships?"

"Yes, sir. They're still about ten hours out."

"Well, contact them and tell them to turn around and go home. The war's over." The man looked confused. "I'll explain it later. Prepare for takeoff." Just before he disappeared in the gap, he turned and looked plaintively at Cullen. "Good luck to you, Mr. Park, but then, I guess you'll make your own, so my wishes don't matter."

Without waiting for Cullen to reply, he turned and disappeared into the shadows.

Charles Ray

TWENTY

"We have a trade agreement with the G'rok?" Moira asked. Her expression was somewhere between happy astonishment and incredulity.

"And, they'll be setting up a consulate and trade mission here on End of the Line," Bitsy said.

"That's right," Cullen added. "And, they'll take as much food and juju juice as we can produce."

"What do we get in return?" Helen Hajib asked.

"Yeah," Larry Jackson said. "What do these lizard men have that's worth the effort?"

"Oh, gold, titanium, iron, you name it," Cullen said. "They live on worlds that don't grow too much food, but are filthy with what they call useless metals."

Eyes got round and the decibel level of

conversation around the council table rose. Finally, Moira rapped a large spoon on the table to restore order.

"I don't know, Cullen," she said. "It sounds almost too good to be true."

Cullen patiently explained the G'rok concept of fighting, and the fact that he didn't think the Saurian capable of telling a lie. Bitsy and Frank supported him with enthusiastic bobbing of their heads.

"Sounds like a good deal to me," Sandra Little Elk, always the most sober member of the council, said. "I think, Cullen, we owe you a debt of gratitude. You have done well."

"By Jupiter, just keeping them dang fops from IDF off the planet . . . no offense, Lieutenant Frank . . . was worth it," Patrick Gonzales said. "They'd be poking their noses in our business, demanding all kinds of service, and trying to get everything on credit. Leastways, the G'rok, being here as diplomats and all, have to follow rules."

Melanie Chang was the only member of the council who didn't seem happy about the state of affairs. "I suppose you're all right, but the fops are human, so it would help my business. I don't see how having a bunch of lizards around is going to help my bottom line."

"Look, Melanie," Cullen said. "We'll be the system trade hub. With the G'rok consulate here, folks from all over will be coming to do business with them."

That brought a smile to her face.

"Oh, yes, I hadn't thought of that. In that case, you have my most enthusiastic support."

Moira rapped on the table again. "It appears unanimous, then," she said. "The council approves the arrangements made by Cullen Park. I hereby move that the council formally thank Mr. Park for his service."

"I second the motion," Jackson said.

"All in favor say aye," Moira said.

Six voices echoed assent.

"The motion passes," Moira said. "Cullen, thank you for your service and for the bounty you're bringing to our planet."

Cullen stood. "You're welcome. Now, if there's nothing else, I have a business to run."

"Wait," Moira said. "We're not done. Now that we'll have an alien delegation here, we need someone to be responsible for dealing with them. Since you're the one who negotiated the deal, and you seem to have their confidence, you're the best person for the job."

"B-but, I don't-"

"And, furthermore," Moira continued, ignoring Cullen's effort to speak. "You did a great job defending the planet, so I think you should remain in charge of defense affairs. I am therefore moving that you be appointed permanent Councilor at large for defense, diplomatic, and trade affairs."

"Oh, I second that motion," Little Elk said.

"B-but-"

"All in favor say aye," Moira said.

"Aye," the other five said loudly and in unison.

"So moved," Moira said. "Effective immediately, Cullen, you are the new Councilor for DDT."

Cullen looked around the table. He saw nothing but smiles, the biggest on Bitsy and Frank's faces. He could hear his grandfather's voice in his head, "*When it's inevitable, boy, just relax. That'll minimize tissue damage.*" He was getting it done to him, and they hadn't even had the decency to ask him to bend over. He would just have to make the best of it. It probably wouldn't be too bad dealing with the G'rok if the others were like K'rket. Unlike the fops from the Federation, with the exception of Frank, he liked juju juice. Compared to Pisante, he wasn't half bad. And, there was always the opportunity as the councilor in charge of trade to make a little on the side. His grandfather had always taught him to be on the lookout for opportunity.

"Okay," he said. "I guess I don't have a choice. Bitsy, you're now in charge of the repair yard. Morley, when you finish your hitch in IDF, how'd you like to be my deputy?" He looked at Moira. "I assume I have the authority to hire staff?" She nodded.

"Well, Morley, whaddaya say?"

"Why, Mr. Councilor, I would be honored." He patted Bitsy's arm. "Now that I'll be gainfully and respectably employed, I guess that makes me a citizen of End of the Line, doesn't it?"

Bitsy blushed.

"Of course," Moira said. "We always need new blood. Our gene pool's a bit shallow."

Frank blushed when the import of her statement sank in. Now, it was Bitsy's turn to pat his arm.

"Thank you, ma'am," he said. "I must say, this has been quite a day. And, to think, a lad from Luna Colony becomes a planetary official, meets new friends, helps to stop a war, and gets to work for the man who will be a hero throughout the galaxy as the man who won the battle of the Galactic Junkyard."

"I didn't win any battle," Cullen said. "Not a shot was fired."

"That's what makes it so neat," Frank said. "They'll write songs about you. You're the first person in history to stop a major war with just your wits. I can hear it now, Cullen Park, hero of the Battle at the Galactic Junkyard. The first war won without firing a shot."

"When you put it that way, it doesn't sound half bad," Cullen said. "What say we go back to my office and celebrate our great victory?"

Charles Ray

Don't miss other fantasy/science fiction stories by Charles Ray

Wallace in Underland The story of a boy who discovers an amazing world beneath the streets of his city.

Chapter One

Wallace Johnson was bored and frightened. Not, mind you, all at the same time, for that would have been more than nine-year-old Wallace could have stood. No, he was bored when he was inside his third-floor apartment with his father Howard. Howard Johnson, a single father; Wallace's mother having died when he was two, meaning that Wallace had hardly any memory of her; worked as a delivery man for a parcel delivery service, and when he was home, he spent most of his time sitting in the living room in front of the TV set sipping beer and watching the sports channel, having little time to do anything with Wallace other than make sure he finished eating his ham and cheese sandwich, which was their usual supper together. On special occasions, Howard would slice the ham thinly and fry it, and spread a layer of crunchy peanut butter on the toasted bread before adding the cheese. Once they finished eating their sandwiches, Howard washing his down with beer and Wallace with cold milk, Howard would go into the living room, flick on the television, and sit there in front of it, only grunting occasionally at something on the screen, before he got up, turned it off, and trundled off to bed.

This left Wallace with little to do when he was

inside. Sometimes he would play with his portable computer game, but he'd mastered all the levels so it was no longer challenging. At other times he'd read, but he only had five books, all of which he'd read so many times he had them memorized. When he had to stay inside, he longed to be outside.

Unfortunately, when he went outside, he longed to be back inside, because that was when he was frightened.

Outside, he more often than not encountered Jamal and his friends. Jamal Henderson was a twelve-year-old who lived in the ground floor apartment in Wallace's building, and he was a bully. When he was with his friends, Melvin Watkins, Abdul Parker, and Delwood Park, he was a tyrant as well as a bully, and when the four of them were together and spotted Wallace outside their favorite activity was beating him up. Delwood Park, a Korean-American who lived in the building across the street with his parents who operated the High's Drugstore on the corner up from the apartments, knew some kind of martial arts and had taught the others. He knew how to pummel Wallace's body, causing it to ache for days, but leaving no bruises or marks; and they never hit him in the face, so he had nothing to show his father after the beatings, not that Howard Johnson would have turned his attention away from the TV set long enough to listen.

On a particularly boring Saturday afternoon, a day that his father didn't have to work, meaning that Wallace had an entire boring day to look forward to, Wallace decided that boredom was worse than fear; at least if he got a head start he could sometimes escape Jamal and his friends, but you couldn't run away from boredom. Boredom clung to you harder than fear, and followed you everywhere you went; from the kitchen to his tiny bedroom, boredom draped itself over his thin shoulders and grasped him so tightly it felt sometimes as if it was trying to suffocate him. No, he decided, better to be scared and try to run away than to be bored and have it stay with you. So, he put his computer game away, kicked his books into the corner, put on his jacket, and headed for the front door.

"Where you going?" his father grunted.

"Outside to play," Wallace replied.

His father grunted something else and turned his attention back to the basketball game that was playing on the screen.

Wallace slipped quietly out the door, pausing just outside and looking up and down the hallway to make sure no one was around. Jamal and his friends liked sometimes to lurk at the bend in the hallway, waiting to pounce on Wallace as he headed for the elevator. Seeing that the passage was empty, Wallace darted quickly around the corner and punched the elevator button. Luckily, the car was empty, and no one boarded on his journey to the ground floor.

The entrance hall of the building was empty as well, and through the glass doors, Wallace saw no one on the sidewalk outside.

Outside, on the sidewalk, Wallace found himself blissfully alone. It was a sultry summer morning, approaching midday, and most folk stayed inside, huddling around their noisy, leaking air conditioners or fans, letting the cool air wash over their bodies. Wallace hoped that Jamal and his friends were doing just that as he headed down the sidewalk toward the corner that led to the vacant lot behind the hulking blocks of brick and steel in which they lived. He threaded his way around shards of discarded newspaper, crushed beer cans, crumpled cigarette butts, and empty liquor bottles that littered the sidewalk in his part of town.

He paused to make sure the weed-dotted lot was vacant in fact before slipping through the space in the fence where two of the gray wooden boards had been removed.

Near the center of the lot, he found the old softball he'd left there the last time he'd come there. Once white, the ball was now scuffed and gray; the lining flapping away in places, and the lacing lose and flapping whenever he tossed it in the air. Wallace tossed the ball into the air and caught it. Sometimes, he'd take a stick he found and hit the ball. He did this again and again. It wasn't exciting; wasn't even interesting; but, it beat sitting alone in his bedroom listening to his father mutter at the television. He wished he had someone his age to play with, but the only other kids on the block were Jamal and his friends, and Wallace didn't like the games they chose to play; usually with him as the object of that play.

He alternated between tossing and catching the ball and gazing at the steel-gray sky, dotted here and there with wisps of snowy white clouds, and the occasional bird that darted through the steamy air to catch the bugs that came out when the weather was hot like this.

Now and then, a stray breeze, cool on his cocoa brown face, would waft across the lot, kicking up little puffs of dust as it traveled. Wallace threw back his head and breathed deeply each time he felt the coolness. From a distance he could hear the dull rumble of traffic on the main street that was three blocks east of the street on which he lived, a narrow, two-lane side street, lined with four and five story tenements, pawn shops, liquor stores, drug stores, and video arcades.

This was Wallace's world; the only world he'd known since he and his father had moved here after his mother died. He didn't remember the house his father said they lived in before, somewhere out in the suburbs on the edge of the city. They'd had to move, his father said, because when his mother died, they lost her income which helped them to pay the mortgage on the house, which was repossessed by the bank when Howard Johnson's income from the parcel delivery service proved insufficient to meet the payments. It was a small world; well, not so small to someone Wallace's size, for he was small for his age; but he knew no other, and at least now it was peaceful.

Peaceful, that is, until his serenity was shattered by the sound of Jamal's nasal voice.

"Hey, guys, it's the punk out here daydreaming again."

Wallace whirled around just in time to see Jamal and his three friends squeezing through the gap in the fence. His heart fell. He quickly went from bored to frightened.

Angel on His Shoulder – Revised Edition   As if Winston Nesbitt's life is not complicated enough, he has to contend with the spirit of his long-dead grandmother who is determined to sort out his life.

Chapter One

Winston Nesbitt's grandmother died when he was twenty-four, and on his fortieth birthday she came back.

She had tried to come back earlier, a week earlier in fact, but her inexperience at being a spirit from beyond the realm of the living, combined with Winston's lack of imagination, had made it difficult. Actually, it had just made it impossible. She couldn't figure out how to get him to notice her. He wasn't the type to notice anything out of the ordinary.

Winston was one of those ordinary people, ordinary to the point of boring. If it didn't fit his normal frame of reference, he couldn't see it, think of it, or believe it existed.

One morning she'd tried getting his attention by flipping the toilet lid closed as he was relieving himself. Instead of attributing it to a ghost or spirit – neither of which he believed in – he figured it was a stray gust of air from the ventilation system. In addition, he'd been so grossed out by the splash of amber liquid over his bare feet, he could think of nothing else as he took his second shower of the morning. A second time she'd rattled the curtains over the window of his bedroom, but he'd blamed that on the wind – he blamed a lot of things on the wind – and had tied the cords tight around them to keep them from flapping about.

She knew how much he loved to eat. Whenever he was upset, he ate. When he was happy, he ate. Winston was a bit on the pudgy side. In an effort to get his attention, she'd hidden in the refrigerator, waiting to say hello to him when he reached in for a snack or beer. That had been a disaster. Spirits aren't supposed to feel anything. Apparently, cold was the one exception. After an hour of sitting next to a six-pack of Heineken, her fingers had turned blue, and she was shivering so hard her clicking teeth sounded like a pair of maracas.

She'd just about given up when she decided to heck with it, she'd just pop into view right in front of his pudgy face and see how he handled it. What she actually thought was, "to hell with it, I'll just scare the piss out of him and see what happens." She would never say that to his face, though, because she knew Winston was a bit prissy about women using dirty language; Winston was prissy about a lot of things.

Now, having your grandmother, or anyone else for that matter, come back from the beyond would be a traumatic experience for the hardiest of souls. Winston Nesbitt was, unfortunately, not the hardiest of souls.

He was in his bathroom at the time. It was 6:30 am, and he was shaving, getting ready to run out to the corner and catch the Number 74 bus to go to the Shady Grove Metro Station to catch the Red Line train and join the thousands of other bored commuters for the long trek to their boring offices in downtown Washington, DC. Preparing for another day just like all the other days, doing the same things he'd done the day before, and would do the following day. Now, just in case you think Winston was bothered by being bored, think again. He knew his work was boring, that in fact he was boring, but he was comfortable with that boredom. It was a predictable kind of boring, and Winston liked predictable. His definition of disaster was when things changed. Boring was good. Unpredictable was bad.

He'd just finished shaving the left side of his pudgy, brown face. He always shaved in exactly the same way; the left side first, then the right, and then the center, doing the space under his wide nose last of all. His routine never varied. Any change to his immutable routine would severely damage his tender psyche.

He was looking like a brown Santa Claus

with half his beard missing. The white foam covered the right side of his face from the curve of his chin to his ears. His tightly curled hair, which he always had cut short, was also beginning to show speckles of gray at the temples, even at the tender age of forty. For reasons that had never been explained to him, all the men in his family turned gray early. He was happy, though, that he at least had a full head of hair, and was not beginning to go bald like a lot of the men his age that he knew. He kept his hair cut short so that all he had to do in the morning was brush it. But, even his hair brushing routine never varied. First he brushed the right side, starting with two downward strokes of the little triangle of sideburn, then straight back ten strokes. He then did the top – ten strokes. The right-side routine was repeated on the left side. Finally, he did ten strokes down the back. Not nine, never eleven, always ten.

Winston lived in a rather sumptuous brick colonial house; two stories with a finished basement that he hardly ever entered; five large bedrooms, each with its own full bath; only one of which he ever used; except for the bathroom downstairs off the sitting room, which he used on occasion. The house was in one of Maryland's wealthiest suburbs. Not the wealthiest; that was in nearby Potomac; but, a neighborhood just outside Potomac, in an unincorporated area that had once been farmland. The farmers, unable to keep up with property taxes, had sold to developers who built overpriced homes that were not quite as luxurious as the mansions in Potomac, but which cost slightly less than the million plus dollars those homes did. Winston's parents had bought the house twenty-five years previously, and sold the small brownstone they'd owned in the District of Columbia. They'd lived there from the time Winston's father had enrolled in the Howard University Medical School. They'd gotten a twenty year mortgage, which was paid off when Winston was thirty-five.

His grandmother had lived with them in the District, and had moved with them to Maryland. She had her own little apartment in the basement, which had been one of Winston's favorite places until he turned twenty. After she died, he never wanted to go back into the basement, and limited his trips to the absolutely necessary, like changing the filter in the furnace. There were just too many memories there for Winston to handle.

The house was in a community of similar houses, just off Dufief Mill Road. It sat just inside the ornate entrance which consisted of two large stone cairns that announced the name, *Potomac Vista.* The name was usually blocked by weeds which the Homeowners' Association could never seem to keep cut, despite the hundred dollar a month fee they assessed every homeowner in the community, and there was no 'vista' of the Potomac, which was three miles south of them. The association didn't take the same attitude toward owners, though. Let a lawn get a bit high and they were all over you;

He had a modest-sized back yard that had once been enclosed by a six-foot-high white picket fence. His father had built the fence for privacy, but had taken it down after a dispute with the Homeowners' Association. Winston had never particularly liked the back yard, but he had liked the fence because it blocked the view from the neighboring houses, and gave him a place of solitude.

Winston didn't like doing yard work. Nor did he like paying the inflated prices to lawn services that hired South American laborers at less than minimum wage, pocketing the difference. He'd considered getting permission from the Homeowners' Association to rebuild the back yard fence so he could let the grass grow and their inspectors wouldn't be able to see it, but decided against it when he saw what a fence cost. So far he'd been lucky. The association hadn't noticed that he never mowed the back yard. Every Saturday during the growing season, he'd take the old lawn mower out of the garage and cut the postage stamp sized front lawn. It was a task that thoroughly tired him out. Just moving the heavy machine from the garage was strenuous, and at the end of the forty-five minutes it took him to do what one of the local teens could have done in ten if Winston had been willing to pay, he barely had the energy to move the mower back inside the garage.

Winston didn't own a car, because he didn't drive, so the mower had the garage to itself except for a few boxes his parents had left stacked against the wall. He'd never seen the need to get a driver's license. Fortunately, the state of Maryland issued a photo ID for those few people who had no desire to get on the Washington Beltway, endangering their lives and others, and this is what he used at the local Seven-Eleven on those few occasions when he had to cash a check in order to have ready cash during the week. The counter clerk at the Seven-Eleven, a skinny Indian from Mumbai who was darker than Winston, always looked askance at the strange man who had no car, but Winston took no notice. The man cashed his check, and that was all that mattered to Winston.

A person of unvarying routine, Winston was severely discomfited by anything that upset that routine. When the wind blew hard, his cable service would be disrupted; and, even if this only lasted for a few minutes, it was enough to send him into a fit of depression, causing him to nearly empty his refrigerator and pantry of anything edible.

He liked things to remain constant, because in constancy there was security.

As a consequence, the appearance of something that in the rational universe he inhabited was not supposed to exist constituted a major disruption of his routine.

He first saw her in the mirror. But, his eyes still bleary from having just awakened, he refused to believe what he'd just seen. One second there was nothing there, and then, there she was. She'd just 'popped' silently into view. Winston had a rapid internal debate with himself. How, he asked himself, does something *pop* silently? It's either silent, or it pops. It can't do both. But, it . . . she had, and that was curious. When he was able to focus clearly things got even more curious.

It . . . she . . . whatever it was looked just like Gran Gran, which was what he'd always called his grandmother, Sally Young. The same caramel colored complexion, high forehead and cheekbones, and the white-streaked hair pulled back in a serious bun. The same piercing gray eyes, that he remembered as a kid, regarding him with that same judgmental expression just before she'd say, "Winston, what's wrong with you boy? You can do so much better." She was always saying that to him, and he'd never understood what she'd meant by it. His life seemed to unfold as it was intended to unfold, so what was the problem?

The . . . his mind was still unable to attach a proper description to what he was seeing . . . had the same wiry frame and reed-thin arms, with rounded shoulders covered by a red and black plaid shawl over a gingham dress, which was what she usually wore. It was the way women dressed in the small Georgia town near Atlanta where she was born, and despite her decades of living in the DC area, she still preferred to dress like they did 'down home.'

The problem with the apparition, and his mind had sort of settled on that as an appropriate word, was that it was only about twelve inches tall. She'd been small, but never that small. Oh, and she was perched on his left shoulder.

He couldn't feel any weight, but there she was, all twelve inches of her, reflected in his mirror, sitting on his left shoulder swinging her right leg back and forth just as nonchalantly as you please. And she *had* popped into view. Not that he'd *heard* the pop, but he'd definitely felt it.

This, his mind finally told him, was impossible. Probably a result of something he'd eaten the night before. So, he closed his eyes and slowly counted to ten. But, when he opened his eyes, it . . . she was still there, looking at him with an impish grin on its . . . her face. He tried rubbing his eyes, but only succeeded in getting shaving cream in his eyes, which stung like the dickens. Rinsing helped the stinging, but the *thing* was still there staring back at him from the mirror.

Winston's brain tried stubbornly to deny

what his eyes were seeing. There's no such thing as miniature whatevers that sit on your shoulder while you're shaving. That kind of thing only happens in B movies that play on cable late at night; the kind you watch when you can't get to sleep. Even in the movies, such things are hard to believe, so no way they could happen in real life.

Whatever this 'whatever' was, it was clearly a disruption in Winston's otherwise orderly if somewhat boring life. His stomach began to rumble as he kept staring into the mirror, and the apparition refused to fade away. It worried him. Not only was it a disruption in his routine, but it meant he was hallucinating, going crazy, or he was still asleep, and having the most realistic and disturbing dream of his life. It didn't matter to him which situation applied, for they were all disturbing. And, when he was disturbed he got hungry. When he got hungry, his stomach made this horrible noise that could be heard from quite a distance.

When he heard his stomach growl it upset him even more. He'd already eaten breakfast. He shouldn't be hungry while shaving. It wasn't part of his normal routine.

Then, he decided to do the one thing he'd so far not done. Instead of looking at it in the mirror, he turned his head slowly and looked directly at his shoulder. And, instantly regretted it.

Sitting there, mere inches from his half-lathered face, was the thing he'd seen in the mirror. Perched on, well, actually, floating about a half inch above his shoulder, now looking him dead in the eye, was a twelve-inch version of his grandmother.

"Good morning, Winston Lee," she said in that reedy voice he remembered so well. "It's been a while. Did you miss me?"

At that point, Winston Lee Nesbitt did what any red-blooded young man of 40 who lived alone, with an unvarying routine, who didn't deal too well with change, and who never did anything more exciting than watch the Fashion Channel late at night in hopes of catching a glimpse of a stray breast, would do when confronted by a foot-tall replica of his long dead grandmother speaking to him first thing in the morning as he was shaving.

He fainted.

Other books by this author:

The Buffalo Soldier series:

Trial by Fire
Homecoming
Incident at Cactus Junction
Peacekeepers
Renegade
Escort Duty
Battle at Dead Man's Gulch
Yosemite
Comanchero
Range War

Al Pennyback mysteries

Color Me Dead
Memorial to the Dead
Deadline
Dead, White, and Blue
A Good Day to Die
The Day the Music Died
Die, Sinner
Deadly Intentions
Death by Design
Till Death Do Us Part
Deadly Dose
Dead Man's Cove
Dead Men Don't Answer
Deadly Paradise

Kiss of Death
Death in White Satin
Death and Taxis
Drop Dead, Gorgeous
Deadbeat
A Deadly Wind Blows
Death Wish

Other fiction

Angel on His Shoulder
She's No Angel
Child of the Flame
Pip's Revenge
Wallace in Underland
Further Adventures of Wallace in Underland
Dead Letter and Other Tales
The White Dragons
The Dragon's Lair
The Last Gunfighters
The Culling
Frontier Justice: Bass Reeves, Deputy US Marshal
Angel on His Shoulder - Revised Edition
Battle at the Galactic Junkyard

Nonfiction

Things I Learned from My Grandmother About Leadership and Life
Taking Charge: Effective Leadership for the Twenty-first Century
Grab the Brass ring

*African Places: A Photographic Journey
Through Zimbabwe and southern Africa*
A Portrait of Africa
There's Always a Plan B
*In the Line of Fire: American Diplomats in
the Trenches*

Children's books

The Yak and the Yeti
Samantha and the Bully
Molly Learns to Share

Charles Ray

About the Author

Charles Ray has been writing fiction since his teens. He won a Sunday school magazine writing contest when he was thirteen, and having his byline on a short story published in a national publication forever hooked him on writing. During his time in the army (1962-1982) he often moonlighted as a newspaper or magazine journalist, and was the editorial cartoonist for the Spring Lake (NC) News, a weekly newspaper, during the 1970s. In addition to his writing, he was an artist/cartoonist and photographer for a number of publications, including Ebony, Eagle and Swan, and Essence, and had a monthly cartoon feature and did several covers for Buffalo, a now-defunct magazine that was dedicated to showcasing the contributions of African-Americans to the country's military history.

After retiring from the army, he joined the U.S. Foreign Service, and served as a diplomat in posts in Asia and Africa until his retirement in 2012. He has worked and traveled throughout the world (Antarctica is the only continent he hasn't visited), and now, as a full time writer, continues to globetrot looking for interesting things to write about, draw, or take pictures of.

A native of Texas, he now calls Maryland

home. For more on his writing and other projects, check one of the following Web sites:

http://redroom.com/member/charles-a-ray
http://charlesaray.blogspot.com
http://charlieray45.wordpress.com
http://www.twitter.com/charlieray45
http://www.facebook.com/charlieray45
http://www.flickr.com/photos/charlesray45/
http://www.viewbug.com/member/charlesray

www.ingramcontent.com/pod-product-compliance
Lightning Source LLC
Chambersburg PA
CBHW060429130626
46555CB00005B/2271